ABOUT THE AUTHOR

'**Indira Parthasarathy**' is the pseudonym of scholar, creative writer, literary critic and cultural historian, Padma Shri **Dr Ranganathan Parthasarathy**. As an academic, he has had a distinguished a career in the Delhi and Pondicherry Universities and the University of Warsaw (Poland). He was the Founder-Director of the School of Performing Arts, Pondicherry University.

As a creative writer, Dr Parthasarathy has carved an enviable niche for himself in Tamil literature. To date, he has published seventeen novels, four collections of novellas, six collections of short stories and fifteen plays. Eight of his novels and many of his plays have been translated into English and other Indian languages.

His novel *Ucci Veyil* (*The High Noon*) was made into a film which won the President's *Swarna Kamal* for the best Indian feature film in 1990. He is the recipient of the Sahitya Academy Award (1977) for his novel *Kuruthip Punal*, the Bharatiya Basha Parishad Award (1996), the Saraswati Sammaan (1999) and the Sangeet Natak Academy Award (2004), amongst many other honours.

Dr Parthasarathy was awarded the Padma Shri by the Government of India in 2010 for his literary and academic achievements.

He has two daughters and a son, and lives in Chennai.

ABOUT THE TRANSLATOR

Chennai-based translator and author Padma Narayanan has translated the novels of Indira Parthasarathy, La Sa Ra, Adavan, Yuvan Chandrasekhar, and the short stories of Asokamitran, Sundara Ramaswami, Krushangini, Cho. Dharman, Dilip Kumar, and the Sri Lankan Tamil writer, A Muthulingam from Tamil into English

She has also translated from English into Tamil, Lakshmi Devnath's *Poorva* – based on the lives of the Vaishnavaite saints and V Sriram's book on Bangalore – *Nagarathnammal*.

Padma, writing short stories since 1954, has been published in many Tamil magazines. She has been contributing articles to *The Hindu* and the magazine, *Eve's Touch*.

POISON ROOTS

~

INDIRA PARTHASARATHY

Translated from Tamil by
PADMA NARAYANAN

AMARYLLIS

AMARYLLIS

English translation of Indira Parthasarathy's Tamil novel *Verpatru*
Translated by Padma Narayanan

This edition first published 2014

AMARYLLIS

An imprint of Manjul Publishing House Pvt. Ltd.
7/32, Ground Floor,
Ansari Road, Daryaganj, New Delhi 110 002
Email: amaryllis@amaryllis.co.in
Website: www.amaryllis.co.in

Registered Office:
10, Nishat Colony, Bhopal 462 003, M.P., India

ISBN: 978-93-81506-44-8

Printed and Bound in India by
Replika Press Pvt. Ltd.

To my parents

1

Nila thunga sthanagiri...

Bhattar's invocatory hymns roused Kesavan up from the stupor of his semi conscious, dream-wake state.

Downstairs, Appa had had his bath, with deference to the early morning chill of the month, Margazhi, had covered his chest with a shawl. In his own inimitable voice, he began reciting the hymns.

Whether Andal's divine compositions had ever succeeded in awakening Krishna or not, he, Kesavan had to get out of his bed now; he had better be up and about before his mother came to wake him up with her affectionate ministrations, he thought.

Kesavan sat up. He had slept rather late the previous night.

An Englishman might have counted sheep to fall asleep. Kesavan, however counted the number of families that lived in the Mantapam nearby.

Peria Komalam was the landlady of that Mantapam. You should ask historians about how she came to own property that belonged to the temple. Or, perhaps, only Lord Sarangapani who resided inside the temple was in the know of things. But there is a story that says that

He had himself usurped the habitat of Someswarar, relegating Siva to a small corner that gave the victim the name Poor Someswarar. Having set such a precedent, how would He ever dispute the claims of Peria Komalam?

Another fact that might have made the Lord wary of action could be the tongue of Komalam. There is a genre in Hindu devotional poetry where devotees take the liberty of singing His praise through indirect words of condemnation; in Komalam's words there would be only abuse, certainly no adoration.

Kesavan could hear Amma coming up the stairs. He stood up and stretched his limbs to mobilise them to action. 'Brush your teeth, drink your coffee and have your bath. Today is the auspicious star Thiruvonam,' said Amma.

Amma rolled up the bedding he had been sleeping on and flung it on the cot. No one ever slept on the cot.

For some time Amma had entertained a desire to sleep on the cot, but soon quelled it. The cot had been around since the days of Appa's grandfather. The then collector of Kumbakonam was an Englishman. He had given this cot to that great grandfather as an expression of gratitude for the Sanskrit lessons the old man had given him. Ever heard of *Murasu* cot described in Sangam literature? This was also one such cot with a mattress instead of a murasu on it.

Kesavan's Tamil teacher, Kovizhiyar, had just the previous week, read out a verse from Sangam period and delivered a 'valorous' lecture to explain its meaning on how the kings of yore showed their appreciation of scholars and poets.

Kovizhiyar's lessons would all appear as if he was equipping the students to go, fight a war. According to him, Indian literature's contention of the basic human emotions arranged into nine categories was wrong; there was only one emotion and that was valour. Once, the learned teacher had roared out the verses that described the fist meeting of Rama and Seetha, protagonists of Ramayana. His fiery recitation had roused a strong doubt in Kesavan's mind: was he talking about the very first loving glances that the couple exchanged or of the subsequent war that Rama fought with Ravana?

Kesavan brushed his teeth and came to sit on the swing in the central hall.

Appa was reciting *Thiruppavai* inside. The aroma of sweet, *Sakkara Pongal* wafted down from the kitchen.

Amma called out to him from inside the kitchen, 'Come, drink your coffee.' Kesavan realised that this call was to let Appa know that his son was up.

He got off the swing and went in.

The combined aroma of incense sticks, sandalwood and jasmine flowers were ushering him into a kind of trance.

Appa was very particular about the religious rites that he had to perform. Yet he never was one to go out in the mornings with the group that went around the streets singing devotional songs. His worship was restricted to his home.

Kesavan went into the backyard.

It was not very cold. The first impact of water is never all that comfortable when you pour the water from the well on you. Then, subsequent buckets of that water on you, makes it become an enjoyable experience.

In the east, the sky looked clear with a few patches of colour patterns.

While he was on his twentieth bucket of water he could hear his mother saying, 'that's enough; don't you drain all the water in the well; be quick.'

He turned around. His mother was standing near the door to the yard.

'I won't be a minute, Amma.'

'I want to ask you something; that's why I'm here.'

'Yes?'

'Where's your *poonool*?'

Only then he remembered.

He was in the habit of removing the sacred thread, *poonool* when he went to college, keeping it in his book shelf and putting it on again after he was home in the evening.

Yesterday he had come home late; he had forgotten to put the thread back on.

'You seem to have lost your tongue!'

'It's not the end of the world, Amma'

'How can you speak like this? We belong to the *Nadathur* clan. What if Appa finds out?'

'So that's what scares you? Don't worry. I'll wrap the towel around my shoulders, run upstairs and become a *Brahmin* again, right?'

'You started college and in no time have got all mixed up. *Saranga*! Put some sense into this boy,' Amma went in.

From the time he started college, all sorts of doubts had assailed his mind. The first one was – caste. And then came doubts about God.

Subrahmanya Iyer, a teacher he was fond of, was about fifty-five years old. A scholar, he had never married. All those who entered the faculty of the college after him had become professors or principals. The rumour was that his independent attitude contributed to his not getting any promotion.

He seemed to have taken a fancy for Kesavan. He would talk about many things to Kesavan. Iyer was greatly responsible for Kesavan's interest in literature. It was not all literature; the master also dwelt extensively on many philosophical concepts in a way that helped the boy get the true implication of them.

These had resulted in Kesavan questioning many things. Indeed, questioning was a sign of intellect.

It did not appear as if Subrahmanya Iyer had other teacher-friends. He was mostly seen alone. Neither did it seem as if many of his students understood the kind of man he was.

His progressive ideas were not based on any political ideology like objection to the caste system or atheism. Neither did he show any interest or involvement in the freedom movement.

'It looks as if our entire nation is engaged in driving away the British. This is only an illusion. We will get freedom anyway – not necessarily because we fight for it. International political situation will take care of it. You know what will happen then? A ruling caste will emerge claiming that they were responsible for winning freedom. This is the curse of our nation!'

Kesavan did not condone his theories. He even wondered at times whether Iyer had regrets about the British leaving India.

Once Kesavan asked Iyer, 'You say that you do not believe in castes. But you have not as yet shed the appendage, Iyer, from your official name.'

'True, I could have had a notification in the gazette and effected the change. But is it all that important? Is it not enough if you feel deeply within you that castes are unnecessary? I know I have that kind of conviction. There is no need for me to make others understand my stand. Look at me; I do not wear the *poonal*. It is thirty years since I got rid of it. At the same time I am not very keen to go and declare to members of the 'self-respect' movement that I am a reformist. This is something personal. I do not hide my opinions under any pretence, not even from my inner self. That's it. Does it make sense to you?'

Iyer's straightforwardness and simplicity drew Kesavan to him.

In the colony that Kesavan lived, they were all Brahmins, with most of them depending on the temple for their livelihood.

The house opposite to his was the temple priest's house and three families lived there. Juicy scandals were being circulated about them all.

Most of the houses on that street had a routine, something like this: all the afternoon hours would be spent playing cards on the thinnais – raised platforms outside the houses; once dusk fell, they would go to the temple to do their respective duties.

When he mentioned this way of life to Subrahmanya Iyer, he said, 'I'll not blame them. Thus have the Brahmin families degenerated. The educated Brahmins become lawyers or government servants. But what will a Brahmin without any educational qualification do? He is not fit to do any work. He cannot make footwear. He cannot get down into the fields and work there. All he is cut out to do is this kind of temple work and spend his leisure hours playing cards. Caste is not a major issue here. Do you know what it is going to be like, once India gets its independence?'

'What do you think will happen?'

'It'll be somewhat like smoking out the bees from a bee hive. The bees will be out in the open with their stings. I do not believe in God, so, I don't know whom to pray to save this country....'

Kesavan stood with folded palms and then took the Prasadam that his father gave him and put it in his mouth.

'Bow down before *Perumal*' said Appa. He bent down to touch the ground and put his hands to his eyes.

'Prostrate properly with all parts of your body touching the ground.' Appa's voice had become louder.

Kesavan did as he was told.

'Ask God to put some good sense in you,' said Amma.

He understood Amma's innuendo very well.

He came to the front door of his house to see if the newspaper had been delivered.

Thalayatti Chakkai, who was on his way to somewhere, saw him and stopped for a moment.

'Yes, Kesava, how is college life? You go regularly, I suppose!'

Kesavan nodded his head. He thought about how the man got his nickname *Thalayatti Chakkai*.

That man's head was always in movement; shaking; so he was a *Thalayatti*. Chakkai was the shortened form of Chakrapani.

Most people of that street had such nicknames: *Peria Mottai, Nadu Mottai* and *Chinna Mottai*....

Periya Komalam of *Mandapam* got her name because among the families who lived in that building, there were three Komalams. How were they to be differently identified?

Since there were four *Aravamudhus* and five *Sarangans* in that street, some such name had to be devised to identify them. In course of time, they forgot their real names and only the nicknames remained.

'What is it, Kesava, I hear that there are more and more self-respect group members in your college, is it true?' asked Thalayatti.

The man's head was in a state of perpetual nodding and his back was bent. He had a dirty towel over his shoulder and his dhoti well above his knees.

Kesavan did not know how that man earned his livelihood. During the temple festivals he took on the role of an odd-jobs man. One of his important duties was to run errands and buy betel leaf, areca nuts and tobacco for the elite who would be playing cards on the *Thinnai*.

Any deaths in the *Agraharam* were occasions for *Thalayatti* to rejoice.

He would not have to worry about his food for thirteen days. Kesavan wondered how at all the preponderance of self-respect groups could affect him.

He did not reply.

'How they hate Brahmins! Did you know that *Rukku* of the corner house could not get her son *Kichchami* admitted into the college and so he just went and enrolled himself in the army? They say that Brahmins have no places in colleges. Your father is, indeed, a faithful, religious man. His good deeds have earned you the merit of a place in a college. How is it with your studies?'

The paper boy came with the newspaper.

Kesavan opened *The Hindu*.

'Yes, that's it. Read *Hindu* regularly, and you'll get to learn good English, they say you don't have to do anything more. That was high school teacher Ramaswami Ayyangar's refrain. So, what is the news in the paper? Everyone claims that we will get independence within a year.'

'Yes, that's what everybody says.'

'You tell me Kesava, what will happen when we get 'freedom'? Is there any way for us paupers to fill our bellies daily? I have heard it said that we'll all get food free and will not have to work at all, is that true?'

'Who said so?'

'You know that lame man – our *Nondi Chakravarthy* – who occasionally speaks at Congress meetings, don't you? He was making this claim day before yesterday at Gandhi Park. Will that come true?'

'How can you get your food without doing any work?'

'What use is freedom if that is not possible? People will become good for nothings listening to this man Gandhi.'

Kesavan saw the futility of continuing the conversation and went inside the house.

Appa was seated on the swing. He did not read the newspaper in the mornings. Afternoons were the time he allotted for it.

Though Appa was popularly known for his traditional scholarship, his English knowledge was the result of his own efforts.

He learnt English more to read the English books that were being published on Sanskrit.

Kesavan felt that his father's sole aim in mastering English language was to write letters to *The Hindu* attacking all those scholars who tried to understand Indian philosophy and ideologies on the basis of their knowledge of Western thought, with little or no familiarity with Sanskrit.

More than half the letters he wrote to the paper got published.

Subrahmanya Iyer once told him, 'I must come and have a chat with your father some day. Why is he so much against English educated philosophy professors?'

'Please don't ever come to my house. One conversation between you and my father will put an end to my college education,' Kesavan said with a laugh.

2

$\mathcal{K}$esavan's thoughts were all about his father even while he was on his way to his college.

Appa's faith in rituals was very strong. By the time he finished his daily routine of ritualistic worship and sat down to have his meal it would be midday. Both Amma and Appa never ate anything until then.

From her talk it was clear that Amma was not wholly in favour of this self-imposed fasting. But she never voiced her dissent and went about helping his father do his pujas.

Kesavan was allowed certain concessions. He could eat the previous night's cooked rice. But he had to come home from college for lunch. Appa had promised Kesavan a bicycle so that he could commute to his college comfortably.

He recollected his early cycling lessons. From what they called 'monkey pedalling', he had graduated to cycling, seated properly on it and was taking a ride through the *Kudiyanavan* lane when he confronted a car coming ahead of him; he swerved to the left to avoid a collision; but only to knock down a man who was enjoying a smoke, gaping at the cinema posters on the wall while easing himself.

The beedi smoker turned around angrily. He was a youth about 25 years old. He sported a thick moustache and his eyes were red. He was bare-chested, covered with lush hair.

Kesavan who had fallen off his bicycle said, 'I'm sorry.' He shouldn't have spoken in English but it was just a reflex action.

The man caught hold of the bicycle with one hand and Kesavan's hair with the other.

'You Brahmin urchin, how dare you?'

'I promise it was no Brahminical arrogance that made me hit you; it was just the most common desire for survival; I didn't want to be crushed to death by a car and so I had to swerve to the left. Please excuse me.'

'Come with me to the police station.'

'You are not all that hurt; then why…'

'So you want to see me hurt badly, is that it? Come to the police station, you Brahmin ass!'

'Forgive me, please. I have no faith in this caste business. Don't call me names taking the name of my caste.' Realising that the man's hold on his hair was slackening, Kesavan released himself from the man's grasp.

'My loss is a *beedi*, thanks to you.'

'I'll buy you two bundles of *beedi*.'

'Right then, leave your cycle here and go, get the *beedi*s.'

'Do I have to leave my cycle behind?'

'Don't you trust me?'

'It's not that. I will be able to get your *beedi* sooner if I go cycling.'

'How am I to trust you? What if you go away home? You sit behind me. I'll do the pedalling.'

Kesavan discovered that smoking a beedi was not all that easy, after he had succumbed to the man's persuasion and had a go at it.

A *beedi* cannot be lit after it is put in the mouth. It had to be first lit and then smoked. It needed some special expertise to see that the *beedi* did not go out in the process.

At the college entrance he saw Murugesan who was a communist. Or at least that was what he called himself.

Murugesan's elder brother was a full-time member of the Communist Party in Thanjavur and had been involved in the farmers' agitation.

Somasundaram had participated in the movement even as a student at the Annamalai University and had courted arrest. Murugesan could only parrot his brother's words and could never put his ideas across cogently and patiently like his brother.

Kesavan very often felt envious of Murugesan. Murugesan would use a smattering of words like bourgeoisie, proletariat, fourth internationalist and other such high sounding words. But whether he used the words, with any understanding of what they meant was worth a debate.

'Comrade, I have something important to tell you,' said Murugesan as soon as he saw Kesavan.

'What about?'

'I heard that your favourite professor was abusing Russia yesterday and you listened to it silently.'

'Number one: he was not talking to me. Solomon, Muruganandam – all fourth-year students – were standing with him. He was talking to them. I happened to go there. That's all. Number Two: What do you expect me to do, even if he does speak derogatively of Russia?'

'Russia stands out all over the world as the symbol of the collective expectations of labourers. Does that country deserve to be rebuked? If Stalin had not been on the scene, Hitler would have made mincemeat of the entire world.' Kesavan looked at him for a few minutes. It was indeed true. If Hitler had not gone to war with Russia, the history of the world would have been something very different.

But, Subrahmanya Iyer's stand on the topic, could not be disputed, either. The treaty between Hitler and Stalin was one that had been forged before the onset of World War II, how credible and just could it be said to have been?

If there was truth in Subrahmanya Iyer's words that Stalin had initiated many killings, was there any wonder that an unbiased question got raised, 'Is the government for the people or the people for the government?'

'Do you know comrade, there is something else as well.'

'Tell me.'

'Subrahmanya Iyer is a British agent. He gets a monthly allowance from the governor.'

'I don't believe it. I have been to his house. Take a look at the frugal life he leads, and you will see no evidence of any governor's allowance there.'

'All the money, perhaps gets deposited in the bank.'

'For whom? He is a bachelor. He has no family commitments. If the British government wanted to help him, it could have placed him in a higher post, why give him a mere allowance? I don't believe what you say.'

'If you don't, that's all right by me. There is going to be a conference of the Zila Students' Federation, perhaps by the end of next month. There is going to be an executive committee meeting next week to discuss this. Make sure you are there.'

'When, next week?'

'Saturday morning Comrade Damodaran is expected to be there. The meeting will be in my house. My parents will be going to Pazhani then to have the tonsure ceremony of my sister's child. My brother might also come.'

'Why, "might"?'

'He was mentioning something about going to Madras. Comrade Dange is visiting Madras, didn't you know that?

'No. I didn't. If Comrade Dange is coming down, then wouldn't Damodaran be going there as well?'

'No, He has promised us that he would attend our meeting. We are planning something big. It is almost certain that our country will be free very soon. What we plan to do after that and how...shouldn't we give some thought to those issues?'

'What makes you so sure about our country becoming independent?'

'That cannot be put off anymore, comrade; Churchill was the stumbling block all along. Now the elections have got rid of him. Atlee is from the labour party. But in capitalistic countries, whether it be the conservative party or the labour party, they are all backward parties. We have to be careful, I gave you a book by Pami Dutt, did you read it?'

'Yes, I did.'

'Good! The Justice party that has donned a new cloak is now talking about social reforms and other such high-flying ideals. But they are also followers of the whites. Only if we are aware of their true colours, will we be able to plan our future course of action,' said Murugesan, letting out gradually the smoke he had held in his mouth.

'I think...,' began Kesavan but stopped midway.

Janaki was walking past them on the bridge. Kesavan thought that as she went by, she gave him a smile. That could well have been only his imagination.

'Hey, speak out man! Say what you meant to say, a casual glance at a female and you become tongue-tied, is that it?' Murugesan's tone showed his anger.

'One should know Marxism; at the same time also learn to worship beauty, right? Only then can he be a complete man,' said Kesavan, laughing.

'If Marx had spent all his time admiring beauty, he would not have been able to write *Das Kapital*,' said Murugesan.

'Have you read the book? I did give it a try. I did not understand a word of it. I think these books are only for us to parrot some quotes from them, not to be read in detail,' said Kesavan.

'You have been thoroughly spoilt by Subrahmanya Iyer. Anyway, let that be. Now Dravida Kazhagam is becoming quite popular among our students. We have to stem this trend. If there were political awareness, say, some knowledge of economic problems, there may not be any need to have a movement for social reform.'

'I am not so sure about that. I think there should be a strong lobbying against caste consciousness.'

'Even if you so desire, the Dravida movement fellows will not take you in their fold. You are a Brahmin. You belong to the group that came into this country through the Khyber Pass and started exploiting the Dravidians,' Murugesan laughed as he said this teasingly.

'Subrahmanya Iyer very often tells me that if I believed in something strongly, I should hold on to it. It is not necessary to convince others of my ideas. And the moment you feel the need to convert others, you become a politician. I think caste differences are wrong. Why should this stand of mine make it important that I belong to any Dravidian movement?'

Murugesan threw his cigarette on the ground and stamped it.

'I am not implying that you become a member of any Dravidian party. I am only saying that you have to be clear in your mind about your priorities. First, the country's independence, then labour revolution.'

Kesavan laughed.

'What amuses you, now?' asked Murugesan angrily.

'You are a romantic, come, let's go. I have my first period with Subrahmanya Iyer.'

They crossed the bridge and went into the college. Kovizhiyar was standing in the veranda. He signalled to Murugesan to go to him.

'Bye, I go my way' said Kesavan. Subrahmanya Iyer was absent. They said that Radhakrishnan would be taking the class.

It was difficult to judge whether Radhakrishnan was young or old. He had an appearance of someone who had become old even as a child.

He had a passion to pronounce English as the Britishers did. Once, when he had to stand in for another teacher, he came to Kesavan's class, wrote on the blackboard the word, Saint John and asked Kesavan to read it aloud. Kesavan read it as it was written; another boy was asked to do the same and he read the word faithfully as it was spelt, pronouncing every single syllable.

Radhakrishnan's ruddy face turned ruddier. He angrily read the word out as San Jon and began to write many such words on the blackboard. Kesavan felt that he would never be sure of how to pronounce them.

Kesavan could not also understand the logic of insisting that English words be pronounced the way the English pronounced them. Did the English pronounce Tamil the way it should be? Where then, was the necessity for any of us to have an inferiority complex or feel bad about our accent, he wondered.

Kesavan felt it would be better to go to the library instead of to Radhakrishnan's class.

When he went to the library Janaki was standing in the English section. She gave him a smile. He had not imagined it this time; she was definitely smiling at him.

3

$\mathcal{K}$esavan could not go to sleep until late that night. His mind kept dwelling on how Janaki, her head bent to one side, had smiled at him and on what she had said that morning at the library.

'I saw you a couple of days back on Extension Road. You were walking with your face turned to the sky; like you were in a dream; what were you dreaming about?'

'I did not see you!'

'I was in the car with my father. We live in the Extension area. You know that, don't you?'

'No, I don't.'

'How come you don't? Half the students in the college know it, they are always seen hovering around the area.'

'I belong to the other half.'

She laughed.

He knew that she lived in 'Extension'. He also knew that her father was a high ranking official of The Imperial Bank of India.

Yet his visits to that area were not with a desire to have a *darshan* of her. He, however, knew where her house was in Extension.

He went to the 'Extension' area to dream. What she had said was, indeed, true.

The fields were on both sides of the road. While he walked around, he would imagine himself to be many different persons; a poet, a revolutionary, a visionary come to save the world.

Shelly was his favourite poet. Subrahmanya Iyer talked about Shelly a lot. At his first year in Oxford, the poet had written an essay on 'The Need for Atheism'. He was expelled from his college for that article. Taking pity on an orphan girl, he had married her. Then he got attracted by Goldwin, the father of Free Love Society and eloped with Goldwin's daughter.

Subrahmanya Iyer would argue that the mistake Shelley had made was to marry a girl out of pity for her. Iyer's stand was that pity should not be the basis for any of your actions. The thought that pity was your motivating emotion would forever be with you, make the action an act of charity. This was negative thinking; so a hurdle for proper intellectual growth.

When Kesavan walked by himself, he would at times become Shelley. He might not have understood the poems well, but he knew more than half the poet's creations by heart...'Clean Map', 'The Revolt of Islam', 'Chensy', 'Prometheus Unbound'....

Janaki must have seen him when he was being Shelly. It was like peeping at someone getting dressed; it was his very private secret.

She seemed to enjoy the fact that more than half the boys in the college kept, 'hovering around' her. He did not like the way she said that. What a cheap thrill she seemed to get; a 'cheap thrill,' that did not go well with her beautiful eyes!

He did not know when he, finally, fell asleep. When he woke up, the sun was peeping into his room.

He went down hastily.

Appa was talking angrily to the uncle from three houses away. In that third house lived five brothers, each one of them living as a separate unit in the same house. The house had seen five generations. One look at it and this obvious fact could be verified.

The eldest was the priest at the Hanuman Temple. The others depended on the Sarangapani Temple for their living. There were three widowed sisters, each under the patronage of one brother.

Appa was talking angrily to the eldest brother.

That man's wife and Amma were standing near the kitchen door. The wife was dabbing her eyes with the end of her sari.

'You a Brahmin and what is all this nonsense? You have a wife, an embodiment of Lakshmi at home, and you go seeking the company of another woman? Are you not ashamed of what you are doing? If you don't give up seeing the "other woman", I'll speak to the temple trustees and you will see what happens to you then! Are you worthy of doing the rituals at a temple where the God, Hanuman, is an eternal celibate? Some name you have, Ramaswami! That Rama was the most faithful husband of all. And you!'

The man pleaded in a feeble voice, 'Swamy, please try to understand...'

'What is it that I have to understand?'

'It is that "other woman" who is maintaining our family.'

'What nonsense is that?'

'My eldest son is a good student. She pays his fees. It is she who helps me get all the functions in my house done. How much do you think I get from the temple? It is a small temple, at the most I may get a rupee a day.'

'To maintain your family you need a "keep"! And you a Brahmin! How dare you confess so openly about it to me? With Brahmins like you around, is there any wonder that they get abused?'

'She's very pious, a regular at Chakrathazhwan temple.'

'Stop this crap. Who is the trustee of your temple?'

'Vakil Aravamudha Iyengar. He and his brother, fighting between them, have competed with each other to swallow all the temple wealth.

Now, the Hanuman in that temple is more or less as impoverished as I am.'

'Stop it, such nonsense will make your mouth rot. Do not talk sacrilege,' Appa shouted in anger.

After this outburst of anger, Appa picked up the newspaper *The Hindu* and went upstairs. As if having kindled Appa's anger was his victory, Ramaswami Iyengar also went out with a smile on his face,

That man's wife Pankajam was moaning to Amma, 'Look how he speaks, Mami, does he ever come home? He is forever at that cussed woman's house.'

'Does she, really pay Uppili's fees?' asked Kesavan.

'Yes, so what?'

'I just asked.'

'What kind of question is that? Just because she pays the boy's fees, will her holding a Brahmin in her house become right?' asked Amma angrily.

'I was not talking about right or wrong, Amma. I just asked if she was paying the boy's fees. That's all.'

As he walked to his college, thoughts of Ramaswami Iyengar's family were uppermost in his mind.

Four of Iyengar's brothers were married. They all had many children.

The fifth was Marudu, real name Varadarajan. He must have been about 25 years, tall and with a good physique....

That Marudu had a liaison with *Konamookku* Sanku's wife who lived in the Mandapam was something that the whole town talked openly about. Marudu was a man capable of all artfulness that required a sleight of hand. He had work to do in the temple during the temple festivals. On all other days he was a proxy for the card players of Town Hall. There was this elite of the town who invested in him and engaged him to play on their behalf. Never in his history of card-playing had he ever lost a game.

The gold chain around Marudu's neck was a gift from the

Udayarpalayam junior Zamindar when he won ₹5,000 for him in a single night.

Devarajan, Ramaswamy Iyengar's nephew was Kesavan's classmate in school. Even getting past the Eighth Standard proved a formidable hurdle to that boy. Try as he would, he was not able to achieve it. He was now employed in the Town hall, running errands, and being at the beck and call of employees there, fetching coffee, betel leaves and cigarettes for them. Occasionally he was engaged in 'private' services for VIPs who visited the town from elsewhere....

It was said that the house Ramaswamy Iyengar and his family lived in, was a bounty from the days of Saraboji Maharaja. It appeared that after the first two generations had lived there, the family had stopped even getting the house whitewashed. The walls were dilapidated. It was also said that an earlier member of that family had done a yagnya in that house and gave the house its name *Dikshithar House.*

The news he heard, when he got to his college shocked Kesavan. Subrahmanya Iyer had been admitted to the hospital. It was feared that he might have had a mild heart attack. The hospital was not far from the college; Kesavan hastened there.

Iyer was conscious. He had a faint smile on his face. He held Kesavan's hand. Kesavan felt tears coming to his eyes. He controlled himself with difficulty.

'I think I've given him the go by,' said Iyer

'Given whom?'

'The Yama the lord of death!'

How was this man able to talk in this manner even now, when he was right at the threshold of death!

'Did you read your father's letter?'

'What letter?'

'The letter that has been published in the *Hindu...*'

'No, I have not read it. What is it about?'

'Looks like a book on Purusha Suktham has been published. It seems there are many errors in the review a scholar has written about it. Condemning the 'very popular man' your father has made some stinging remarks.'

'How does that help anybody?'

Subrahmanya Iyer put his palms to his ears.

'There is a materialistic culture that claims that only useful things have the right to exist in this world, go, become a member of that group,' said Iyer.

'What is wrong with that?'

'You dare ask if there is anything wrong with that line of thinking? I am just glad that I will not have to live in an Independent India.'

'Iyer, no talking!' the doctor was coming in.

'He is my favourite student. He says that things that are not of any use have no right to exist in the world. The first casualty to that line of thought should be me!'

'I did not mean that. What I was trying to say was....'

'Please, no argument.' The doctor said as he began to examine Subrahmanya Iyer.

Murugesan hurried to him, as soon as he was back in the college.

'Where were you? I was looking for you.'

'I had gone to the hospital, to see Subrahmanya Iyer. Do you know that he has had a mild heart attack?'

'No, I don't. You are contesting the student union election. I wanted to tell you this.

'What are you talking?'

'The Congress men have their candidate, as do the DMK. We have also to participate, you will contest the post of Joint Secretary of the union.'

'This is a decision I should make.'

'No. my brother has sent word that it should be so. You have to stand for the election.'

'Look here, I cannot do it. Number one, I do not want to. I do not want to be in the limelight, right under all those eyes. Number two, I do not like the political parties making its entry into college elections.'

'Hey, some preacher you are! Do you believe in Marxism or not?'

'What does belief in Marxism have to do with student union elections?

'Oh, yes, there is a connection. You have to contest the election.'

'Why don't you stand for it?'

'Anna has ordained that you should be our candidate. He has immense trust in you.'

'Look, Murugesan, Please leave me out of this.'

'No way, a party that made its appearance only recently, the Dravida Kazhagam, has put up a man. How can we not have one to represent our party?'

'Your choice of candidate will make their win easy.'

'How?'

'I am a Paapaan – Brahmin, remember?'

'Who sees you as a Brahmin? Let us see if anyone brings that issue up. If you win, that will be a great blow struck at castecism. Perhaps, Anna suggested your name, only because of it.'

Kesavan stood there, his mind all in a muddle.

4

*K*esavan was thoroughly ashamed of himself.

He wanted to run away from Kumbakonam.

He had lost the election. In addition to the Dravidian party candidate, Kittu from the Student Congress was also a contestant. Kittu had told him before the election, 'Just withdraw. If you don't, the Brahmin votes will get divided and Chokkalingam will win.'

Kesavan had felt rage well up within him. 'I do know all these racist politics. I was wondering if I should get into all this, now that I see you take this line, I sure am going to be part of it. Let Chokkalingam be the winner; I don't care.' But Chokkalingam did not win, either.

Now, he was an 'also ran'. What would Janaki think of him?

'Communists are the slaves of the British. They were not with the Congress during the Independence struggle in 1942, but on the side of the whites'– this was the argument that the Congress candidate had to say against the Communists.'

Kesavan tried to justify his party's stand. 'Hitler was the common enemy. To preserve a civilised world, he had to be opposed and so one had to be the allies of the British.'

Kesavan, however, realised much later that their problem had nothing to do with the British or Hitler.

Kittu was the 'minor' of Mavur. He threw money around lavishly and all his supporters benefitted economically.

Kesavan had a doubt that Janaki would have also canvassed for Kittu. But there was no clear evidence to substantiate this misgiving.

Murugesan put all the blame for the failure on Kesavan. 'You should have gone and met the voters individually. I had to go on your behalf. But, did that help? Kittu went and met each and everybody personally.'

'Didn't I tell you that I was not at all fit for elections! But you would not pay any heed.'

'Forget it, you fool. Nothing is lost as yet. Let's wait for the next election.'

'I promise this – no more elections for me.'

'You certainly are not fit for politics. You say you've read Marx and Engels and yet when it comes to action you turn tail and run away like a coward, are you not ashamed of yourself?'

'I don't remember having ever heard of Marx or Engels contesting any election.'

'Be a cynic, that's all you are fit for.' hissed Murugesan.

The one positive offshoot of the election was that people in the college came to know of Kesavan's existence in the college. At least 38 would have become aware of his presence. The votes he got were 39.

Chokkalingam who was the Dravida Kazhagam candidate spoke to him after the election results were announced. 'I have also lost; but that does not bother me. I expected I would get 250 votes. All the promised votes went to Kittu. Those who voted for you were also our men and that for the sake of Murugesan. I am telling you all this, only to make you understand how corrupt your race is.'

'As far as I am concerned there is no my race or your race; I know of only one, the human race.'

'Yes, I agree, all are humans. Why did not the Brahmins vote for you? Kittu is a cheat, a rich playboy, who has money to throw around. You are a good man, a communist. And yet, they did not vote for you. Do you know why?'

'Tell me.'

'Other Brahmins are afraid of a Brahmin who claims that all castes are equal, that's the real reason.'

Subrahmanya Iyer was on a long leave. He would not have known anything about the elections.

Or that was what he thought. When Kesavan went to see him after having lost in the election, he was reclining in an easy chair and welcomed him with a smile, 'Come on, election hero.' He realised that Iyer knew all that had happened. He felt a sense of shame.

'I was told that you were standing for the election and also that you were not doing enough canvassing. They said that you did not shake hands with anybody and everybody to ask for their support; plead, "vote for me." They say that this was also a reason why you lost. Look here, once you decide to contest an election, you should have put aside all your self-consciousness and pulled all the stops to win. You cannot expect to have the cake and eat it too,' said Iyer.

'It was a mistake that I ever got into it,' said Kesavan

'That's something you say now. That only shows your lack of conviction about anything. In fact...'

'Yes, go on, please.'

'This courage of conviction...I don't think it will be possible for any of you to have it, once we become free.'

'Why do you say that?'

'Mmm. You ask me why? Now this Independence is for whom? Only for those who say, "You have swindled the country all these days, now it is our turn." This is what has happened in each country after it became free. Human behaviour never changes. All the hue and cry about conviction, ideals and the whole works will disappear as soon they sit on the seat of power. As the ruler, so the people – the Sanskrit saying goes. I will not be around to witness it. But you will. You will then understand all that I am talking about now. But if you become a politician yourself, what chance then that you'll remember me? Don't mind what I said, that was just a thought.'

Kesavan's father did not know anything about Kesavan having stood for the election or having lost it.

Amma sensed that her son was in low spirits.

'Anything wrong with you?'

'Nothing, Amma.'

'She put her hand on his forehead. He removed it.

'I tell you I'm alright,' he said dispiritedly.

'Don't bathe in cold water. Take a hot water bath.'

'I was playing for a long time yesterday. So I'm just tired. Don't make a big issue of it.'

'You played? That's news! When you were at school your drill master, Jagannatha Iyengar, would come home to complain that you never went anywhere near the playground at all.'

'That was then. Now I play cricket.' With these words, he went upstairs.

He had not gone to the college for a couple of days after he had lost in the election.

He would leave home and go straight to the 'Gopal Rao Library'. The librarian there liked him.

A well-read man, he would find any book that Kesavan asked for. Why so learned a man like him continued to rot there for a pittance, was an eternal mystery to Kesavan.

It was from that library that he had borrowed and read all the Balzac novels.

'Read, just read whether you understand them or not,' librarian Vaidyanathan had said earlier.

His advice proved useful to Kesavan. He was the one who had suggested that Kesavan read Balzac.

He felt like crying after he had read, Balzac's *The Quest of the*

Absolute. He did not know why he felt like this. It was a story about a scientist who tried to find God in a laboratory.

When he mentioned this to Iyer, he said, 'Going in search of God is in itself a sob-story. Didn't all our devotees cry their hearts out to see God? Devotees search for Him inside their hearts, the scientist looks for him in his lab. That's all the difference there is.'

'But, why did I cry?'

'I am afraid that you are becoming a devotee as well. There is no difference, whatsoever, in being a communist or an ardent devotee.'

'What do you think is wrong with Marxism?'

'Nothing is wrong with Marxism. Only because he had compassion in his heart Marx could write the *Das Kapital*. Look what has happened now. If only Stalin had been as compassionate, would he have indulged in the massacre of lakhs of people? Not just Marx, this is what happens to all great men. That's the irony,' said Iyer.

Vaidyanathan asked Kesavan straight away. 'These past two days, you have been coming here, no college?'

He told him what his problem was.

'Don't be a fool, go back to your college. Nobody is going to be bothered about your winning or losing a stupid election,' said Vaidyanathan

When Kesavan went to college he saw how true Vaidyanathan's words were.

No one said anything about the election or about his losing the contest. The hot topic under discussion everywhere was the murder of a rich landlord Ganesayyar, who owned three houses.

Kesavan had not read the newspaper that day. If he had had, he would have also been aware of the murder.

He had never heard of Ganesayyar. But the way the students were talking about him, it appeared that the gentleman was a popular figure of the town. Going by what the students said, it looked as if he must have had a concubine in each one of Kumbakonam's streets. That rich he was said to be. Kesavan could not quite understand if the students were lauding the gentleman for his sexual prowess or condemning him.

Ganesayyar had a relationship with a woman next door to his house. She was about thirty years old whereas Ganesayyar was more than fifty-five. She also had a liaison with a young tailor who had his tailoring unit in the front veranda of her house. Ganesayyar did not know about this secret connection, between the tailor and his lover. He also owned the house where the lady lived. It was, he who had permitted the young man to have a tailoring unit there. When he came to know of the secret alliance, he got the young tailor tied to a tree in his garden and thrashed soundly.

Ten days later, the tailor had his revenge. They said that he severed the head of Ganesayyar sleeping on the third floor of his house, leaving it attached to the body by just a hair's breadth.

There were contradictory opinions that the tailor might not have committed this crime. Actually, Ganesayyar had any number of enemies who could have done it.

The one proof cited to establish that the tailor was the murderer was that he had put the young granddaughter sleeping by the side of Ganesayyar, on the floor before he murdered the older man.

People spoke about how his having spared the child made one infer that the tailor had a kind heart; they were least bothered that this rumour was evidence enough to hang the tailor.

Kesavan felt a vicarious desire to see the body dangling by a hair's breadth.

The boy who had reported to Kesavan about this said, 'You should have gone in the morning to see the gruesome sight. Now the police refuse to let anyone inside the house. I heard about the murder at six o'clock this morning and went there immediately. The body was hanging like a puppet. It would not have if the thread that had held it had been slack. Blood was all over...making designs on the floor.' When Kesavan went to his maths class, half the number of students were not there. However, the teacher was there.

Kesavan had always wondered how Sambandam Pillai ever came to become a maths professor. He was always seen in three-piece suits and that too a different one each day. It was a favourite pastime of the students to guess how many suits the man owned.

There was absolutely no resemblance to anything Kesavan had imagined a maths professor to be and the real Sambandam Pillai. He had formed a mental picture of someone with a tuft, a turban, a dirty long coat, shod with an old pair of slippers, with a forehead adorned with a caste mark with a habit of being irritated all the time.

The first day Sambandam Pillai came to his class, Kesavan thought he was the English professor. When that gentleman began teaching mathematics, Kesavan was shocked.

It was said that he was very rich and even owned a car. For him teaching was only a pastime. He was an ace maths teacher. It was just a pity that Kesavan was not any good in the subject.

Kesavan's interest in the class was to watch a man sitting outside the room and tugging at a rope to which a banner made of cloth, *punkha*, was attached. It circulated air just above the master's head.

The expense of engaging someone to pull the '*punkha*' was to be met by the concerned teacher. So, many teachers did without this luxury only to sweat profusely while taking their classes.

The man who pulled Sambandam Pillai's punkha was an old man, a retired peon. Just because the man had a large family of nine children, Sambandam Pillai pitied him and had engaged him for the job.

The punkha would be moving in full force at the beginning of the session. The speed would come down gradually and at a certain point stop altogether.

Snores would be heard from outside the class.

The old man's head would be seen nodding while his hands pulling the rope would have stopped moving.

Sambandam Pillai was quite aware of this habit of the punkha-man. He would stop his lesson midway and smiling, take a peep outside and then glance at the punkha. He would then begin to raise his voice by several decibels and speak even as he continued to write on the blackboard.

'The square on the side of any triangle is equal to the sum of the squares on the other two sides less twice the rectangle contained by one of these other side and the projection of the second side upon it.'

The spirited chanting of this trigonometric theorem would wake up the old man sitting outside.

The punkha would, once again start moving fast.

This was an interesting experience of the maths class for Kesavan.

Sambandam Pillai saw Kesavan in his class and told him, 'You are a murderer, too. How come you are not interested in Ganesayyar's murder and you are here at my class?

'I, a murderer? What do you mean?'

'Yes, a murderer of maths. Do you know how many marks you got in your last assignment?' He opened the bundle of answer papers he had in his hand.

'I know it, sir. Please don't read out the marks in the class,' pleaded Kesavan.

5

$\mathcal{K}$esavan was sitting on one of the benches in the playground, feeling a deep sense of dejection. The reason for his feeling so low was his wondering about how he would ever successfully tackle the task of crossing the formidable ocean...the ocean that mathematics appeared to be.

Kesavan's mathematical prowess gave Sambandam Pillai many occasions to exhibit his sense of humour. Sambandam Pillai would say something like 'If "Zero" was India's contribution to the world of mathematics, then it must have been one of Kesavan's forefathers who invented it.' It would take at least a couple of minutes for the wave of laughter that would break out in the class to subside; many more such jokes were made at his expense.

He felt he should not have ventured to study mathematics. Appa had forced him into it. Though the mathematical genius Ramanujam had once lived on that street and that too not very far from his house, belying Appa's belief, no wind of mathematics seemed ever to have blown his way from the house of that genius.

The result of his scoring centum in his SSLC exams, though he himself was not sure how he had achieved that, was Appa's trust in his abilities, Sambandam Pillai's endless jokes and his present dejection.

Marker Lawrence came towards him.

'What's it, *Thambi*, you sit here looking as if you have lost the whole world?' asked Lawrence.

Lawrence was very tall, with ash-coloured eyes and a fair complexion. Generations of his family had been markers in that college. People talked of some connections Lawrence's family had had to one of the earlier white principals of that college. That would, perhaps, account for his ash-coloured eyes and fair complexion.

'Tell me, *Thambi*, why are you silent?'

'Nothing.'

'Your mouth says "nothing", but you sit here as if all the cares of the world are on your shoulders. Tell me, what is your problem? Didn't you get selected in the cricket team?'

'I am considering discontinuing my studies.'

'Why so, *Thambi*?' asked Lawrence as he put his hand on Kesavan's shoulder.

'I am absolutely no good in mathematics. It's too late now to drop the subject and take another one...without getting through my maths exams, how am I ever to complete my college education?'

Lawrence laughed loudly.

'Do you have to laugh at me, now?' asked Kesavan irritated.

'Who is the swimming champion of our college today?' asked Lawrence.

Kesavan could not understand what the college swimming champion had to do with his miserable attempts to master mathematics.

He silently lifted up his face as if asking, 'Why this question?'

'Just tell me,' said Lawrence.

'Williams.'

'Do you know how he became the champion?'

'I don't. How?'

'Good, I'll tell you how. Just as maths scares you, the Cauvery waters scared him. His father Herbert is related to me; he was a good swimmer, a great leftwing football player as well. His son and scared of water? I just couldn't take it. One day, I bundled the boy and threw him into the water, saying, swim, you mother-fucker.' That was it. That day on, all his fears were gone. Today he is the champion. Thambi! Who teaches you maths? Is it the castor oil Ramachandra Iyer? '

'No, it is Sambandam Pillai.'

'What are you cribbing about, then? He dresses in style like a white man, his teaching is so good.... You find maths difficult even after he has taught you?'

'You mean to say a well-dressed man will definitely be a good maths teacher?'

'Oh, yes, there is a connection between the two. Doesn't his name Sambandam mean connection? Do you know why the boys call Ramachandra Iyer castor oil? His traditional wearing of a dhoti, his dirty turban, his coat with its colour all-faded, thick streaks of sacred-ash on his forehead, and grumbling all the time...shouldn't a man look impressive?'

'Do you know Sambandam Pillai?'

'Very well. He has a butler in his house like any white man. Flush with money, he is. He can have any number of servants. What he earns as salary in the college is not enough even to buy his ties, he has so many!'

'Can you do me a favour?'

'What?'

'Sambandam Pillai makes fun of me in the presence of girls because I am not good at mathematics.'

'Oh! That is your problem! In the presence of girls! Tell me which girl specifically! Give me money for a bottle of rum, for sure I'll finish the deal.'

'No, I am not interested in any girl. I am only interested in my studies.'

'I was joking, my dear. I very often go to Pillai's house. Generous man, he gives me drinks, English stuff. I shall put in a word to him at the appropriate time. Challenge mathematics, you will win,' said Lawrence.

Kesavan felt somewhat heartened by this conversation

The bell rang. The third period. It was Kovizhiyar's class.

Someone said he belonged to the Dravidan party. Sometimes it would appear so when he attacked the Brahmins subtly in the class.

In his class there was a boy called Krishnamachary. He had tuft and the Vaishnavite caste mark adorned his forehead.

Once, he got up as soon soon as the bell rang.

Kovizhiyar said, 'Yes, Krishnamachariar, you seem to be in a great hurry to go to your "Aam",' with special emphasis on the word, "Aam" a term used by Brahmins for 'home'.

The whole class laughed.

This did not mean Kovizhiyar was a Dravida Kazhagam man.

He did not seem to have the athestic stand of Periyar. A great devotee of Muruga, his examples would all be from *Thiruvachakam*, spoken with utmost devotion. Kesavan knew that Kovizhiyar had a soft corner for him. This was not just because Kesavan was good at Tamil; there was yet another reason too. The first time Kovizhiyar came to teach Kesavan's class, he had asked each student to speak about their favourite lines from Tamil Poetry.

At school, Kesavan had had to study, *Oorchoozhvar*. He had learnt the entire portion by heart and discovered that it was steeped in emotion. As he recited ten lines beginning with *'Enranan Veyyon,'* Kovizhiyar's face brightened.

'Where is this extract from?

'Silappadikaram.'

'Who is the author of *Silappadikaram*?'

'Ilango Adigal.'

'Do you know the entire *'Oorchoozhvari'*?'

'Yes, I do.'

'Why do you like this particular portion?'

Kesavan was not able to specify why he particularly liked that part. He was not sure if it would be a proper reply if he said, 'This portion is so emotion-packed.'

'Tell me,' Kovizhiyar asked in a louder voice.

'Because it is packed with emotion,' Kesavan drawled.

'Good! That's the right answer. It reflects the frenzy of a woman to whom injustice has been done, very like a humiliated race rising up in anger now.' He continued his diatribe.

When Kesavan entered the class, he saw Kovizhiyar was already there. He hesitated near the door. Kovizhiyar turned his head and saw him.

'Haven't I told you all that I do not want my students to come to my class even one minute late?' asked Kovizhiyar. Kesavan stood there silent and with head bowed.

'Ok, go to your seat.'

Kesavan could find a seat only in the last row. Who was this, sitting next to him? He must have been around forty; dressed in a dhoti and black coat; hair dishevelled....

Kovizhiyar also noticed the gentleman only then.

'Who are you?' growled Kovizhiyar.

'I have heard that your classes are interesting; so I thought I would sit in.'

'You should have first asked my permission. Anyway, it's alright. My aim has always been; as the saying goes: "may everyone enjoy what I have found pleasurable." What is to be today's lesson?' Kovizhiyar asked the students.

'*Thirumurugaarrupadai,*' one of the students in the first row piped in.

'Right; A lesson on *Ennai Alvonai* – One who rules over me. *Arrupadai* is the work of a staunch Tamilian, Nakkeeran, who had the gumption to find fault in Lord Siva's composition and declare, 'An error is an error even if it made the culprit angry enough to open the third eye on his forehead.'

The man sitting next to Kesavan mumbled something.

Kesavan could not hear what the man said.

'In those days, the Tamils were so valiant that they never shied away from armed wars as well as wars of words. Valluvan has emphasised this in his Kural, 'Even if you were to be the enemy of one who wields weapons (bows), don't ever become the enemy of one who wields words.' When the red-haired, God found that he could not win over his opponent by his verbal arguments, He got angry and opened his third eye to intimidate His rival, a Tamil poet...'

Kesavan's neighbour spoke loud enough now, for him to hear, 'Nakkeeran was my elder brother.'

What was he babbling? – Kesavan looked at him, slightly taken aback.

The man laughed.

'What makes you laugh?' Kovizhiyar's voice thundered.

'*Thambi* is clueless,' said that new man all the while laughing.

'What does he not understand?'

'Who Nakkeeran is!'

'Don't worry about that. Kesavan is my student. You do not have to teach him who Nakkeeran is!'

'Do you know who Nakkeeran was? Tell me.'

'What kind of a question is this?'

'Look man, don't call me stupid and all that. I'll get angry.'

Kovizhiyar's eyes reddened in anger.

'Get out!,' thundered Kovizhiyar.

'You tell me who Nakkeeran was, and I'll go my way,' said the man as he stood up.

Kovizhiyar was at his wits end.

Kesavan felt that the students were trying to control their laughter. Kovizhiyar was well-known for his anger.

Kovizhiyar had immense faith in his ability to teach. It was his firm belief that no one could could resist being awed by his craft of expression that made words pour out of him, undammed. There were a few occasions when outsiders had come to his class to listen to him.

'This is not a compliment paid to me. Mother Tamil sits on my tongue and speaks through me. What right do I have to stop others from benefitting from such divine speech?' Kesavan remembered how his teacher had been rather modest about it all. He proudly told his students that this was the same explanation he had given the principal when the head had objected to allowing outsiders into a formal class. He had proclaimed then, 'People are jealous that the eternal sweetness of Tamil language attracts people from all over.' None of those who had come to listen to him had ever claimed Nakkeeran to be his brother, though. Neither had anyone questioned who Nakkeeran was.

Now somebody was asking that question. Though angry at first, Kovizhiyar decided that it would be prudent to pacify the man with a reply and said, 'Keeran was a great poet who belonged to the group who shaped conches. The prefix 'Na; denotes his greatness. Are you satisfied now? Go out, please.'

'Who wants all this explanation? Do you know that Nakkeeran was my elder brother?'

The students could not control their laughter anymore.

Kovizhiyar got down from the platform and walked towards the man.

Kovizhiyar was not less than six feet tall. He had a physique that could come in handy in 'body-building through regular exercise' advertisements. To quote from his favourite literary work, *Kamba Ramayanam* 'Allaiyandu Amaintha meni – a body that measured the dimensions of the earth'.

Kesavan trembled.

He looked at the man sitting by his side. The man looked as if it was years since he had had something to eat; he looked an exact blueprint of an emaciated poet described in ancient works like Aatruppadai. The man was swaying. There was not an iota of fear on his face. Kesavan thought that the possibility of Nakkeeran being this man's brother could not be completely ruled out.

'Who are you?' asked Kovizhiyar calmly.

'Brother of Nakkeeran.'

'Right! Now you go out.'

'No, I'll not go out even if you open the third eye on your forehead. I'm Nakkeeran's brother, remember? I am not someone to be taken lightly.'

Kovizhiyar went near the man and put his hand on the scruff of his neck.

A student intervened at this juncture. He was Panneerselvam, a BA final year student. A sportsman who regularly won prizes in many sprinting competitions.

'Sir, please, I'll take him out. Don't mind him,' said Selvam.

'Who is he?' asked Kovizhiyar.

'My uncle, he gets soused up and behaves like this. Chithappa, come with me…. What's all this?' said Selvam

'Selvam, you tell him who I am…' said the man, as he went out tottering.

'I'll do that. You just come out now.'

The class was silent for a while after the two had made their exit. Kovizhiyar was staring into vacant space. Then he said, 'You may disperse now. No one should speak of this incident outside this class. If I come to know that someone has, I'll squeeze his life out of him.'

6

'*K*esava...'

Kesavan was not sure if Appa was calling to him or just chanting one of the twelve sacred names of Vishnu.

That the tone was in a mode of addressing someone was made clear when he called out again, 'Kesava!'

Kesavan came down.

'You are not ready to go? Be quick,' said Appa.

'Go where?'

'What question is this? Have you forgotten that today is the day you change your sacred thread, *Avani Avittam*?' Amma spoke.

Amma had bathed and stood there pure enough as the occasion warranted.

Kesavan was thrown completely out of gear for a minute. The primary reason was that his sacred thread was upstairs, not on him as it should have been. The second terrible thing was that a group of Brahmins, led by his father would be setting out from their Sannidi Street to the river Cauvery. If it was the first *Avani Avittam* after someone had been initiated into wearing the *Poonool*, then the rigmarole would be much more. It was mandatory that they all walk towards Cauvery River with a Nadaswaram party leading the procession playing their instruments, and those reciting Yajur Veda following, all the men bare-chested, each with a pot and a smaller container, silver or copper according to their respective economic status.

Last year he could go through it; no one was as yet aware of his 'progressive thinking'. But today, after having had expressed his line of thinking quite overtly, how could he make the journey to the river almost a mile away from his house? What if somebody saw him?

He would not be able to get away with the excuse that he was doing it, because he was scared of his father. Murugesan lived near Melakkaveri. If he saw Kesavan in that crowd, bare-chested and all, he might ask, 'you too, Kesava!' in a Julius Caesar tone.

The Nadaswaram could be heard at their door, many voices calling out, 'Mama' as well.

'Let me do it at home,' said Kesavan

'What do you mean?' thundered Appa.

'I'm not coming to the Cauvery.'

His father glowed red in anger. Rage choked him and did not let words come out.

'You're not coming...to Cauvery...why?' his lips quivered. This was a new experience to him. Generally, if he was not happy with some of the things that Kesavan did, he could quell his son with just a stern look. But this defiance was something new; here was the boy announcing clearly that he did not want to come with them to the river to do the ritual!

Outside the crowd had gathered. Some of them were reciting Thirupallandu spiritedly.

This was an experience, rather new to Kesavan as well. Until then, he had never gone beyond the initial line of protest against his father. His father's searing looks would burn away all his grumbles. Today he had declared, though in a feeble voice, 'I am not coming to the river.'

Like the mediating country caught between the Allies and the Nazis, Amma stood there trembling and looking at them alternately.

Appa, usually used the fourth strategy of warfare, *Dandam* or the threat of the rod. Realising, perhaps that that strategy might prove ineffective, he resorted to the second rule, conciliation....

'You see them as your friends, well-wishers, but they really are your enemies. Remember that. If you'll not follow the prescribed caste rituals, then you are equal to an animal. As much as you aver that you have no belief in this hierarchy of castes, they'll never forget that you were born a Brahmin, remember that. Now, just come with me.'

Appa's advent into this new strategy shook Kesavan a little. He stood there for a few moments, silent. 'Hm...mm...come, they are all waiting for us.'

'I don't proclaim that I am against castes to please somebody. I really believe in what I say. If the others will not forget that I am a Brahmin, what am I to do?' said Kesavan.

'Kesava, what's wrong with you? Is this the way to talk to your father?' asked Amma in a feeble voice.

'Let him talk, let him. Doesn't our proverb say that once they, your own sons, stand taller than you, they are your friends? If he has decided to go the way he wants to, I can also do the same. Perhaps he has decided that he can do without a cycle. If he wants to haul himself everyday to college, make it on foot, let him.' This was another strategy of war, offering sops.

After Kesavan's one-day trial to master the art of cycling looked like it would escalate into a huge caste-war and a truce was achieved through the bribe of a 'beedi', he had stopped pestering his father to buy him a cycle. Now Appa was coming forward with that offer. The price he would have to pay would be his 'progressive thinking'.

Why expect Murugesan to come from Melakaveri to see him at the river doing the ritual? Che! Was the problem only about Murugesan misunderstanding him? The truth was that Kesavan did not believe in these rituals. This was the right moment to make Appa aware of it.

Appa will have to be shown that he could be firm in his conviction even at the cost of forfeiting a cycle.

At that point, 'Three Cards' Chakrapani Iyengar came in. He was the uncrowned king of the 'Three Cards' game. The moment he collected his cards, his co-players would shout, 'three aces!' It was widely rumoured that he played proxy for Neduntheru 'Junior Minor' Seema.

'What is the contention between father and son?' asked Chakrapani

'He says he doesn't want to come. Let's go.'

Appa was not keen on letting a third person interfere in his family problems.

'And, why won't he come?'

'I do not believe in these empty rituals,' said Kesavan

Appa glared at him.

He said, 'Come; let him be.'

'No, that's not the way to deal with him. Let me talk to him. What is the reason for your disbelief? Are you a member of that self-respect group?

Kesavan was considering whether it was at all necessary for him to discuss in public his political and social stands.

'Tell me now, Kesava, I know all those self-respect fellows. This Vakil Narayanasami Odayar will speak at length as if he is one of the foremost disciples of Periyar. Yesterday I was at Oppiliappan Koil. Who do I see there, but this Narayanasami's wife and children? It was his turn to sponsor yesterday's rituals. He was not there, must have kept away because it would be such a shame if someone saw him there. They talk, that's all. You must come with us, if you have any respect for your father's words, even if it goes against your personal beliefs. Everyone on this street respects your father for his scholarship. And you question him? That's enough, stop all these arguing and just come with us.'

'Kesava, g...o,' Amma's voice sounded as if she was almost at the point of breaking into tears.

Kesavan looked at his mother.

His fortress of opposition got demolished before her look of love and anxiety. He went upstairs to put on his sacred thread and came down, ready to accompany them.

Appa lead the group, chanting Vedic verses. The others followed repeating them.

As Appa's son he had to walk with his father, right at the front bearing the silver pot and tumbler. There was no way he could escape public eye.

As soon as they came out of their house, Appa said, 'Uppili, take the vessels from Kesavan, walk with me in the front.'

Uppili was the eldest son of an Iyengar who was the cook at the Hemarishi Mandapam. He was at school, a very good student, doing his SSLC. He had also studied the scriptures the traditional way.

Happily Uppili came forward to obey Kesavan's father, and put out his hand to take the vessels from Kesavan's hand. His 'knowledge' had found acceptance. He had earned the right to walk alongside Kesavan's father!

When Kesavan handed over the vessels, happy and relieved, Uppili felt a sense of disappointment.. He expected Kesavan to demur while his father would get angry with Kesavan. What thrill could there ever be in easy victories!

Instead of Vedic verses Appa began to chant the introductory verse of *Thirupallandu*, the celebrated work of Alwar.

'*Gurumukhamandeeya Praahavedana Seshaan*
Narapathi Parikluptham Sulkamadanu kama...'

This sent a wave of surprise all around. Uppili also did not expect this. He wanted Appa to see how good his pronunciation of the Veda was. He could recite them with proper stresses on the right syllables.

Kesavan walked at one end of the last line of that group.

His efforts to hide his sacred thread with his towel over his shoulders could not refute the fact that he was walking to Cauvery with a group of Brahmins.

As they went past Gandhi Park, Rajamanickam saw him from his photo studio and hastened towards Kesavan. Kesavan tried to pretend that he hadn't noticed Rajamanickam.

Rajamanickam was a very poor student while at school. After he came to college, he suddenly was seen sporting rings on his fingers and a chain with a tiger-claw pendant around his neck. The secret for this sudden flush was revealed only later. He had married this Christian nurse some ten years older to him. That was the story behind Siva Rajamanickam's metamorphosis into Peter Rajamanickam.

Rajamanickam came up to him on his cycle. He had a smile that mocked Kesavan.

'What is it comrade? Where are you off to?' He laid special stress on the word, 'off to' saying it in the Brahminical dialect.

Kesavan did not reply.

Appa's stentorian voice continued with the Alwar's verse.

Rajamanickam continued his attack as well.

'What is it comrade, you go by without giving me any reply?'

Kesavan repeated a line from the verse that was being chanted; it meant 'we'll not let those who serve their stomachs and fulfil only their material needs into our group'.

'What are you saying?'

'That was the reply to your question. '

'I don't understand.'

'I don't expect you to, Mr Peter.'

'Your comrade disguise is all gone up in thin air, exposing your *poonool*, Mr Kesavan.'

'Why are you going so slow on your cycle, as if you are participating in some slow-cycle race? Leave your cycle at Somu's shop there and come, join us. If you want I'll throw a sacred thread around your neck as well...'

'Tell me if I'll get something by having it on, and I shall be only too ready,' said Rajamanickam laughing.

'It had its uses once upon a time, not now. You see what trouble it gets one into and yet you'll have it?'

'I, certainly, have no such desire. You made me an offer and I laid down my terms. Let that be, why are you in this predicament?'

'I do believe that I might even be up to driving the whites away from this country; but my energy to stand up to my father seems to be rather limited. Moreover, as you just now suggested, I am to get some benefit out of this action.'

'What do you expect to get?'

'I have been promised a cycle if I go through this ritual! Something, perhaps, like what induced Siva Rajamaickam to become Peter Rajamanickam..'

'You are buying a cycle? Will you buy this cycle from me? It is new; from Singapore. Look at it, complete with dynamo and all! Has it even lost its shine?'

'Why would you ever want to sell it?'

'I'm buying a motorbike. Mary says a real man will ride only a motorbike.'

So, then what will a cycle rider be?'

'Stop this silly talk. Tell me if you are interested; I shall give it to you for its cost price.'

The chanting voices suddenly stopped. Appa turned to look at Kesavan. The others in the group followed his gaze.

Kesavan and Rajamanickam realised that they were the centre of attraction.

Rajamanickam hesitated. He was debating whether he should stand his ground or leave the place at once. His departure might mean that his cycle will not get sold. Since it was an expensive bike, he was finding it rather difficult to get rid of. Those who could afford such a cycle were all Muslims who could get another new one straight from Singapore. Rajamanickam knew that Kesavan belonged to a well-to-do family; a well-to-do family not really familiar with the quality and price of cycles, though.

Uppili ran to Kesavan and told him his father wanted him.

Kesavan walked up to his father.

'Who is that boy?'

'My classmate.'

'Why do you walk, talking shop? Shouldn't you concentrate on whatever it is that you are doing?'

I was concentrating on my conversation with him – for a moment, Kesavan toyed with the idea of giving this reply

'He has a cycle shop. He has some cycles, imported from Singapore; very much in demand. He was saying that I should go immediately to the shop, if I wanted one.'

'Call him here.'

Uppili went on the errand once again.

Rajamanickam came, looking scared.

'Did you say that you had a cycle for sale?'

'Yes, Sir.'

'What's the price?'

'360 rupees, it has a dynamo, and then....'

'Ok, ok, come home and do the talking. Don't do your trading business in the middle of the road. Give respect to whatever business you may be doing, understand?'

'Yes, Sir.'

Appa picked up the chants from where he had left off.

7

$\mathcal{K}$esavan stood, in front of Murugesan with bowed head.

This gesture of shame was the response to Murugesan asking him, 'Are the reports I heard true?'

Kesavan could very well guess what Murugesan might have heard.

Kesavan's new Singapore cycle was the hottest topic of discussion among students. Even the breaking news that the dialogue between Lord Mountbatten and the Indian leaders had been successful (Gandhiji had moved away from the discussions because he could not accept the country being divided on the basis of religion, and he didn't want to be a spoke in the wheel of the country achieving Independence) and that India was about to become free, did not attract as much attention as Kesavan's cycle. What was of more interest to the students was that Kesavan had chanted *Gayathri* and sported a new *poonool* to get the cycle.

Rajamanickam had spread this 'hot' news among the students.

Murugesan did not expect one of the student leaders, Kesavan, to indulge in such an act of treachery, especially, just when the conference of Tanjore Students Federation was about to take place there.

Murugesan's question and Kesavan's look of contrition would become clearer when seen from this angle.

'You have let me down miserably, flogging me down as it were, in front of all those boys from the Dravidian movement. And here is my brother suggesting that you be made the leader of the conference reception committee,' said Murugesan.

'No, don't even suggest that. I don't want to be any leader,' said Kesavan.

'So you care more for donning your sacred thread, is that it?' asked Murugesan raising his voice a little.

'It is no use my talking to you. There's no way you are going to understand me,' said Kesavan.

'What is it there to understand? Tell me, did you or did you not get the *poonool* on your back?'

'Yes, I agree I did that. I needed to have a cycle before the conference began.' How else would I be able to run around doing the various errands that I might have to? If I were to get the cycle, I had to have this thread on. Only then would Appa let me buy the cycle. Hasn't the great Engels himself said that to attain one's goal, one can adopt any means?'

Murugesan glared at Kesavan. He did not know whether Engels had ever spoken those words or not. But, seeing Kesavan quoting him with such authority, he felt the economist did, perhaps, say that. Yet, he was not prepared to give in so easily.

'Engels gave those comments under different circumstances,' Murugesan said, the words coming out with some hesitation.

Kesavan could make out that Murugesan was not sure of his ground. He persisted, 'Come on. Tell me what those circumstances were.'

Chinnayyan, who had all along stood there a silent witness to this dialogue, butted in with, 'Enough of this argument, Murugesa, Kesavan has a point. He does not believe in wearing a *poonool*. What great calamity can happen if he puts it on to please his father and get his cycle? Let us talk about other things that need to be done.' Murugesan was silent for a few minutes. He looked as if he was trying to ingest the truth behind Chinnayyan's words.

'The cycle will not be just yours. It will be the common property of the conference. Anyone will have the right to use it any time. Agreed?'

'Agreed. But I don't want to lead any reception committee.'

'No way that decision can be revoked. They are my brother's instructions. We have to, first, get the fliers printed. Our stand has to be made very clear to the students. You make a draft of the script and bring it with you this evening. We shall have a discussion on it then.'

Just then Rajamanickam came there after hauling up his new motor cycle on its stand.

'*Vanakkam* Comrades!' he said. The slight mockery in his voice did not escape them.

None of then responded to his greeting. They must have decided that it would be prudent to ignore him.

Rajamanickam did not belong to any particular party. But it was an open secret that he helped the Dravida Party Students' Association financially.

'I hear that you are going to convene a conference,' said Rajamanickam.

'Yes,' said Murugesan.

'Kadirvelu told me that Kesava Iyengar is to be the chairman of the reception committee.'

'Rajamanickam, you are a fraud. You came to my house, nodded to everything my father said to sell your cycle to us. What right have you to take this mocking tone now?'

Murugesan intervened, 'Keep quite, Kesava.' Then he turned to Rajamanickam and went on, 'All that Kesavan did was to wear that *poonool*. But, remember what you did? You married someone ten years older to you and why? Only to get your motorcycle that you have parked there. What right do you have to talk about anybody else? If you don't mind your business and leave this place, I will get wild.'

Murugesan's anger was rather well-known. Rajamanickam who

was also very well aware of this, laughed and said in a conciliatory tone, 'Murugesan, no need to get worked up that much. I was just joking. Kesavan is my friend as well. Kathirvelu told me that there was talk of a conference; so I asked you about it. Anything wrong with that?'

'Then, why the damn do you call him Kesava Iyengar and all that?'

'I'm sorry. If your conference needs some money, tell me. I'll help you.'

'Go, give it to the Dravida Kazhagam. I don't need any of your money,' said Murugesan.

Chinnayyan butted in, 'How can you be so rude, Murugesan? He is offering us a donation. What's wrong in accepting it?'

'Look here, I don't belong to any party. I will give the Dravida Kazhagam money and I'll also help you. They don't have any faith in temples or Gods. I go to Church regularly, every Sunday. I am a believer, I do not conform to their views.'

'You'll starve, if you don't do your Sunday Church ritual, right?'

'I did change my religion to become rich, I accept it. But after I came into this religion, I read the Bible and am now convinced that His path is the right one. This is the truth. I promise. Don't ever have any doubts about it,' said Rajamanickam.

'Ok, how much will you give us?' asked Chinnayyan.

'Ask, and it shall be given.'

'We'll talk about it later, you leave this place now,' said Murugesan.

The bell rang announcing that it was time to go to their classes.

'It is my English class, now. Professor Sabesan knows my father. There is no way I can skip his class. Let us meet at Gandhi Park this evening,' said Kesavan as he hurried to his classroom.

Professor Sabesan would have been around forty-five years old. He had got his promotions rather quickly and was now the head of the English department.

He was always clad in suits. There were varied rumours, some saying that he was 'England Returned' and others refuting the claim saying that he was merely putting on airs.

After hearing him speak English, it was difficult not to accept that he might have been in that country. There was also talk that Right Honourable Srinivasa Sastri had appreciated the way Sabesan spoke the language, English. The opposition parties however, contended this claim.

Ramu, who lived near Sabesan's house once said that the professor dyed his hair black.

'They say that there is a black dye. You apply it on your hair and it makes your hair stay black; but you have to repeat the procedure once a month,' Ramu had said.

Kesavan thought that there could be some truth in what Ramu said.

Otherwise how could Sabesan's hair stay that dark? It didn't look like it was a natural colour. One look at it and it proclaimed, it was different. It didn't appear as if oil could have given it that kind of sheen. Sabesan and Kesavan's father shared a unique kind of friendship.

He had come one day to Appa and told him that he was keen on studying the Vedas and the philosophical thoughts they contained.

Kesavan's father had said, 'There are any number of books in English that speak of these things. Why don't you read them?'

'It is said that no amount of reading will be equal to learning it from a master. You teach me, I'll come to you once a week,' Sabesan had said.

Appa would also read aloud to Sabesan the manuscript versions of the letters he wrote to the various newspapers and journals and hand them over to the professor. Sabesan would take them to the college, get them typed and forward them to their various destinations.

Sabesan did not know the name of any of his students. He called them all, 'Son.'

But he knew Kesavan by name.

When Kesavan came to his class Prof Sabesan was already there. 'Come in, Comrade,' greeted Sabesan. Kesavan's discomfiture was evident. When Kesavan had sat down in his place Sabesan asked him, 'Yes, Comrade, tell me who wrote the book, *Illusion and Reality*?'

Kesavan stood up. He had never heard of such a book.

'Christopher Caudwell! What sort of a Marxist are you that you don't know even this fact?'

8

*K*esavan got tired of looking for it in the entire college library. He did not find the book, *Illusion and Reality* anywhere. How could the head of the English department who had not got the book for his own library accuse Kesavan for not being a true communist just because he had not read the book!

It was then that the Truth dawned on him. That was Marxist literature. It would need some special courage to stock that book in a government college library operating under the all merciful British rule!

Librarian Jagannathaier asked him, 'Is that such an important book?'

Jagannathier must have been about fifty years of age. He had a sizable tuft, with hair that had not yet showed any sign of greying. He sported both holy ash and Kumkumam on his forehead; he was said to be a follower of the Devi cult. Though he did have a Masters in Philosophy, he had not chosen to become a teacher.

'Professor Sabesan said that it was a good book,' said Kesavan.

Jagannathaier called him, 'Come here,' lowering his voice.

Now what secret was this man about to come up with?

'He is a phoney, humbug; he reads all those "bad" books.'

'Yes?'

'Oh, yes! Have you heard of DH Lawrence?'

'*Lady Chatterley's Lover?*'

'Yes. The same man who wrote that book. He has kept that book for the past two years, he has not brought it back. The book, he has suggested that you read, must also be one such. He dyes his hair, what a fake he must be! Be careful.'

Kesavan looked at him sharply. Why was this man so much against Sabesan?

'You stick to your course books. That's enough.'

Perhaps, *Illusion and Reality*, was, to use the librarian's language, a bad book! Was Sabesan making fun of him?

Kesavan went to Subrahmanya Iyer's house that evening. He was sitting in the hall, poring over a manuscript, straining his eyes. He was on a long leave.

'Welcome, comrade,' teased Iyer.

'What manuscript is this?

'It is the handiwork of your professor Kovizhiyar.'

'What is it about?'

'He has set the verses of Homer's *Iliad* in Tamil metre '*Parrodai venba*'. He has asked me to go through it and give him my comments.'

'How is it?' Without giving any reply Subrahmanya Iyer just smiled.

After a few moments, he said, 'Tell me about you, how are you?'

'Have you read the book *Illusion and Reality*?'

'Christopher Caudwell, a Marxist scholar, a very intelligent man who died very young. A good book certainly, but needs some effort to read it.'

'Professr Sabesan asked me in his class if I knew of this book. I said I did not. He laughed at me as he said, 'What kind of a communist are you that you have not even read this important book.'

'Do you think that man has read the book?

'I don't know.'

'I told him about the book. He said that he would get it for the library. But he hasn't yet got down to do that. He is scared to get a Marxist book for the library. His next promotion will make him a principal, get it? His fears are understandable.'

'Where can you find that book?'

'Go. Look in that cupboard, seventh book on the third shelf. Read it and return it safely. You may not understand all of it, but make as much as you can of it.'

Kesavan picked up that book. He marvelled at the man's memory that knew precisely where each book was in his cupboard.

'Don't you begin to circulate the book among your comrades. Take care to return it promptly, understand?' said Subrahmanya Iyer.

'I didn't expect you to have Marxist literature,' Kesavan smiled.

'I don't see Marx as a communist; He was a *rishi* like Charvaka. Only when you look at him from a historic perception can you ever understand him. When the Industrial Revolution erupted in Europe, the emergence of a Marx was inevitable; this is a compulsion of history. Perhaps, it is because such inevitables keep occuring in history in almost all fields of knowledge, that Einstein said, "God does not play dominoes". I seem to be the one doing all the talking, you tell me, what brings you here? Bring some water from inside and then tell me about it.'

Kesavan went into the kitchen.

Everything was in astate of disarray. He did not know which pot contained drinking water.

There was a mud pot in the corner of that room. He tilted the pot to pour some water into a glass and brought it over to Iyer.

'I took this from the mud pot, I suppose this is good water,' said Kesavan.

'Don't you worry, I shall live long. I have given *Yama* the slip once. If he comes anywhere near me again, I shall start talking of Marx, Engels, Freud, Einstein and he will take to his heels, never daring to approach me again,' said Subrahmanya Iyer and laughed.

'Aren't all the others except Einstein already there? Yama seems to have had the courage to face them all, hasn't he?'

'No, our *Yamaloka* has no place for Jews. It is only because they feel that they do not have any special place of their own, that they have spread all over the world. They should thank Hitler for their being able to claim now that they will create a separate country of their own after the war. Hitler massacred thousands of Jews and now the world's sympathies are all with them.

'How is it that Hitler claimed Germans were the real Aryans?

Subrahmanya Iyer laughed.

'Why do you laugh?' asked Kesavan

'Don't you see some half-baked people nearer home, ignorant of both history and culture, claiming that the Brahmins are all Aryans and the rest Dravidians? Hitler's contention was something similar. Do you know, how many of our stupid Brahmins believing in Hitler's words, began to pray that Hitler should win the war? I, sometimes very much like Ford, see "History as a garbage bin". Sometimes I am with Hegel who has elevated history to the level of something sacred. I am a prisoner of all my contradictions, doubts. No exit or salvation for me, ever.'

'I remember your having told me that doubts at least constant intellectual questionings, pave the way for a human being's growth,' Kesavan reminded Iyer.

'There is a Kural couplet that goes:

Than those of grateful heart, the base must luckier be

Their minds from every anxious thought are free

'Do you know the meaning of this verse? If you don't, ask Kovizhiyar.'

'You tell me now.'

'We, generally, understand the word 'Kayavan' – a base human – but Thiruvaalluvar is supposed to have used it here to mean an evil person. I, however, feel Valluvar refers to a philistine, has used a word that probably refers to the "funny (strange) people" of Bharathi.'

He appeared to be talking to himself. His eyes were closed. He looked quite exhausted. Kesavan felt he should not tire him any further.

Though his eyes were shut, his mouth was murmuring, 'Doubts are my bane, my hell. Hell, heaven...what am I blabbering about? To

accept Milton's words it is the mind that decides Hells and Heavens.
Yes, he is right; he is right.'

Kesavan though Iyer must have gone to sleep.

He came out, shutting the door noiselessly.

When he came back to his college, he saw Murugesan hurrying
towards him.

'Where were you? I have been looking for you the entire morning –
fliers, receipt book, everything is ready. Here, take them.'

Murugesan took out a bundle from his shoulder bag and opened it.

The fliers had been printed in red.

'What is this?' asked Kesavan.

'What else? They are the notices about our conference.'

Kesavan saw that it contained a paragraph opposing the British
dictatorship, the next one on Indian capitalism and another with
varied suggestions to do away with castes...all written in an alliterative
language that spewed fire.

At the bottom of it all was the signature 'Kesavan, President'.

'Hey, what's this? Why have you put my name here?'

'Aren't you the president?'

'So what? I would never ever have penned any flier in such words.'

'This is the style of writing that attracts people nowadays. That is
the style that is making the Dravida party popular.'

Kesavan was running his glance over the written material – A
famine in the rice bowl Thanjai; a government that beds with famine; –
'What's all this nonsense? How would a government bed with famine?'

'Beds?'

'Yes! What else? Doesn't the Tamil word '*manjam*', used here
mean cot?'

Murugesan was quiet for a few moments.

'How many of these have you printed?'

'A thousand.'

'And the cost?'

'I've not yet paid the printer. I got them printed in our comrade Kannappan's press.'

'Let us do this, get some new ones printed. Tell Kannapppan that we'll make the payment later and get some new ones printed. Right?'

'I had asked Nandagopal, because he was good at Tamil, to draft this notice. Who would have thought that he would bring in words like bed and cohorting? When he read it out to me, it sounded nice. You mean to say that these thousand fliers are a waste?'

'Absolutely! Get your brother to read this and see how angry he gets. Haven't you read Jana Shakthi? Do they write in this style?'

'OK, then. You bunk your class now. Draft a new one. Come, let's sit near the Canoe Club and get it done. You will be able to do a good job if you sit on the banks of the river and write it.'

'Is this some poem that I am to write to get my imagination flowing by sitting on the banks of a river? It is just an announcement that makes your intentions clear. I'll write it at home and bring it to you tomorrow morning. I will be able to express myself well, only when I sit and write it at home.'

'If you put it all in your Brahminical language, no one will read it. What guarantee is there that the ambience will not influence your writing?' Murugesan asked laughing.

'If ever my ambience had any influence on me, I would be here tuft, caste-mark and all, chanting *Gayathri mantra*.'

'Oh, yes, don't we know that you did all that chanting to get your cycle! Anyway, make sure you have your draft ready by tomorrow morning. Just one more point. Stick to whatever ideas are expressed there. Change only the style. The contents have all been suggested by Annan. If you changed any of that, Annan will get angry.'

'This is a student convention, but none of the problems that students face have been mentioned. And, you have said that representatives from all socialist countries will be present. Are they all really coming here?'

'Annan said they were coming. Look here, you are not allowed to change any of that. Just put these ideas in some simple language that everyone will understand, that's all you have to do.'

When Kesavan got home, Ramabhadra Iyengar was sitting on the swing. A six-foot tall man with a physical frame that matched his height with a prominent caste mark adorning his forehead, he had retired after faithfully serving the His Majesty as an engineer. Now he spent his time tirelessly talking about the advantages of the Imperial Rule to the world at large. He had a nickname, 'the white Alwar'. It was worth looking into whether this name was given to him because of his loyalty to the whites or because his complexion was not dark.

'They have flung Churchill off, these stupid British people. Would they have done it if they had an iota of gratitude in them? Now, what is Atlee in power, achieving? He has promised to make all colonies free. Now what will that mean? Haven't the people of our country already let the pariahs into our temples? Who knows what else we will be witness to? Have the whites ever interfered in any of our religious practices?' Iyengar was in his element, letting off steam.

'You, genius! How are your studies going?'

Kesavan was irritated. He went inside without answering the man.

'Look at him, walking away, ignoring my question! Would any such thing have happened in olden days? We had some humility, some respect for the elders. Now the old and the young are all equal; husband and wife are equals, the Brahmin and the pariah are equal.... Only God knows where this country is heading to!' Kesavan could hear Ramabhadra Iyengar's laments. He went straight into the kitchen.

'Have a wash, I'll make your coffee,' said Amma. 'Why is this man here, every single day, torturing us?' Kesavan asked. Amma looked at him angrily.

'How can this daily praise of the whites be tolerated?' said Kesavan

'Because he served the whites, he has been able to acquire a couple of houses on Patrachar street, two on Iyengar street, one in the Extension and one on our street. What is wrong with his adoring the whites?' said Amma in a soft tone.

There was no mockery, whatsoever, in Amma's voice. Hers was a traditional behaviour pattern that saw the benefits accrued from devotion to God and loyalty to the whites on par; everything should yield some kind of benefit; what does it matter to whom you owe your allegiance? What was important was that devotion should shower positive results. Devotion and loyalty were important....

Kesavan was not sure if Appa even condoned Ramabhadra Iyengar's opinions. Appa listened silently to all that Iyengar mouthed. Appa needed Iyengar's help; on the vacant plot next to Iyengar's, he was building a house.

9

Kesavan was up at six and when he came down early, his mother looked at him with wonder. 'You seem to have come to your senses,' she said even as she put her sari out to dry on the clothesline tied quite high above her.

She had the red towel tied around her wet hair, an indication that she had had her bath.

Kesavan remembered what occasion it was only when he saw a very old man, dressed in the traditional style, entering their house.

It was his grandfather's death anniversary.

He now understood why his mother had praised him. But his getting up early had nothing to do with the ceremony that was to take place that day.

He had to go to the railway station. The party leaders were coming from Chennai and in his capacity as the president of the conference he had to be at the station to receive them.

Murugesan had told him the previous day. 'Come to the station at seven in the morning. I'll get the garland. Don't come late and give me some lame excuse. Understand? I say seven, make it seven sharp.'

Kesavan would have just enough time to have his bath and leave for the station. But now with his grandfather's impending visit in the offing, will he be able to get away and go to the station? What reason could he offer his father?

The conference began that day. He had to be there to render the welcome address.

All national leaders of the party like Manali Kandasami, Selam Damodaran, Mohan Kumaramangalam, Parvathy, Baladandayutham were coming there.

What a pity that *Thatha's* death ceremony had to be today!

How could he ever get out of this tangle? Appa came in, ritually 'clean and pure', after having had a bath at the well-head in the backyard.

'Don't go to college today, Have your bath soon; chant the *Gayathri* at least today.'

'I have to go to college today,' said Kesavan in a firm voice. He was surprised at the determination in his tone.

'Why?'

Appa looked straight at him.

'There's a function at the college today. Many well-known professors from other cities are attending it. Since my English is good, the principal has asked me to give the welcome speech. I have now to go to the station, receive them and take them to the principal's house.'

Appa stared at him for a few moments. It was not clear from his look if he believed Kesavan or not. Or was he wondering if his son was all that clever to be delegated the responsibility to receive all those great professors?

Appa walked silently towards the kitchen.

Kesavan was surprised that his father had accepted his statements so very easily.

He had his bath, got dressed and was about to leave the house when he heard his father call him.

Appa who was engaged in setting up the Saligramam to be ritually worshipped asked him, without turning to look at him, 'Who are the professors coming?'

Taken aback at this unexpected question, Kesavan answered after a minute's hesitation, 'I think they are all professors of English.'

'Who?'

'Prof Chacko, Prof Menon, Prof Kedari Rao,' Kesavan went on to list a few, carefully mentioning only Malayalam, Telugu and Kannada names. He was taking the precaution to avoid Appa recognising any of them.

Appa got up from his seat.

'OK, I'll talk to Sabesan; you don't have to go to the college.'

Kesavan broke into a sweat as soon as he heard Sabesan's name. How could he have not foreseen that Appa was sure to talk about this to Sabesan?

He was not happy at the way he was piling up lies one after another.

He remembered the conversation he had had earlier with Subrahmanya Iyer once on his predicament. Iyer had said, 'If you believe in something, you shouldn't worry about whether it is acceptable to others or not. Your father may not approve of your convictions. If you do not have the courage to face his opposition, just be one of the herd. Don't ever mouth high-sounding cliché phrases like, 'I've an individuality, I've an independent mind' and all that.

The time had come for him to stand up to his father.

'All that I told you now are lies,' he said. Appa did not reply. His silence was ominous.

'What is it that you have been lying about?' asked Amma, worried.

'This is no college function. I am not going to the station to welcome any professor. Today there is going to be a convention of the Students' Federation. All the leaders of the Communist Party are going to be here. I am going to the station to receive them.'

He felt a rush of relief after he had made this confession.

Amma looked at Appa.

Appa was silently wiping the puja vessels dry, with a white cloth.

Kesavan walked towards the entrance.

'Kesava!'

Amma came after him calling out to him.

'I am scared, Kesava.'

'Scared about what?'

'Appa's silence.'

Appa's silence had unnerved him as well. But he did not want to overtly show his discomfort.

'I have to go Amma,' he said, in a conciliatory tone.

'Should you go even after you have been told that it is your grandfather's death anniversary?'

'I am the president. How can I not go?'

'Will you come home for your lunch?'

'How is it possible, Amma?'

'Alamelu, come in, don't go begging him to do this or that. Let him go.' Appa's voice came out loud. Amma went inside the house, muttering, 'Do what you will.'

Kesavan was at the station right as the train was coming in. Manali Kandasami, Salem Damodaram and Baladandayutham were the three who had come by that train. They were told that the others would be driving down. Murugesan told him that his brother Somasundaram who had initially said that he might not come, had come the day before.

There he was introducing the students to the leaders.

Kesavan was very much taken with the way Baladandayutham spoke. There was both refinement and clarity in it.

'Why has comrade Mohan not come?' asked Murugesan.

'Mohan has been travelling a lot. We tried to buy him a first class ticket by this train, but we couldn't get it. So he's coming by car.'

'Are you sure, he'll come?' asked Somasundaram.

'Very sure. He'll be here by lunch time. Isn't his speech scheduled only for this evening? Is there somebody among your students who can translate well?' asked Manali.

'Whose speech needs translation?' asked Kesavan.

'Comrade Mohan's, his Tamil is not all that good. His English, however, is so good that it will put any Englishman to shame,' said Somasundaram.

The oft-repeated words of his English teacher at school, Rangachariar, came to Kesavan's mind. 'You must all learn to speak English like Valangaiman Srinivasa Sastri. Englishmen admired his English and listened to him attentively. His oratory was, indeed, wonderful.'

Kesavan wondered if only the list of leaders who could speak English well were long enough, there would have been no need at all for any other form of struggle for independence. He believed that the way Indian leaders like Nehru, Patel, Rajaji, Jinnah and others had communicated effectively in English with Mountbatten had brought the day of Independence closer.

Subrahmanya Iyer often said, 'Blame it all on our inferiority complex.' Sastri found a grammatical error in the English that Churchill spoke. Do you know how that was enough to make all our Mylapore Mamas go into raptures? There Hitler was bombarding the country; this was a life and death situation for the British. Churchill spoke a few words to boost the morale of his countrymen. Our scholar was able to find errors in that speech. That made us revel in our superiority as if we had rocked the foundations of the empire.'

'Why are you silent? Say something,' said Murugesan to Kesavan sotto voce.

'This Thambi is the president of our conference committee. He is very good at both English and Tamil,' said Somasundaram, patting Kesavan on his back.

'Then, let this Thambi translate Mohan's speech into Tamil,' said Manali.

'That was exactly what I had in mind,' said Murugesan.

Kesavan saw this as a new hurdle. The morning had already begun with the problem at home. Now this issue of being an interpreter... he was well aware that he was no public speaker. He had prepared an eight-page welcome address and had memorised it. He never could speak fluently like Kovizhiyar or any Dravida Kazhakam student leader. How then, was he to manage instantaneous translation of Mohan's speech?

Mohan had had an English education; he could speak so well as to put many a Britisher to shame. Understanding his words and immediately expressing them in Tamil...would he be able to do it?

The conference was to be held in a medium-sized building near the railway station. It belonged to the brother-in-law of Balu Rao, the president of Kumbakonam Bus Workers Union. It was neither very big, nor very small. It had three rooms where the leaders could rest.

They had erected a *pandal* in front of the building. Two hundred chairs were put in there; if there were more people attending the conference, they would have to stand.

The building also had a large central hall. Lunch was to be served there.

Only when he reached the conference venue, did Kesavan realise that the number of students present at the venue was meagre – not more than thirty. The labourers had come in hordes with their entire families. The conference pandal was bustling with tots of all ages. The kids who were having a ball, playing around the posts in the pandal, stopped their running around and looked at the leaders with awe and curiosity.

It was Comrade Balan who first realised that there were not many students present.

He asked Kesavan, 'Aren't you the student head?'

'Only the president of this conference,' said Kesavan.

'Never mind that. What's the reason for the number of students being so few?'

'They'll come,' said Murugesan, still not losing hope.

'How many members are there?'

'About a hundred,' said Chinnayyan.

'The town is quite big, accommodating so many schools, and this college, an ancient one, with 400 students on its rolls, you say you have a membership of hundred. Does it speak well of your organisational capabilities?' said Balan.

'After this conference, more students will join us,' said Murugesan.

'There are not many students here. How will they join?'

'Comrade, what does it matter if the students are not there? The labourers are here in good measure. Don't talk to these students so discouragingly and dampen their enthusiasm.' said Manali.

'The Student Congress is more powerful here, then come the Dravida Kazhagam, we come only after them,' said Kesavan.

'And why is that?'

'It could be because the student federation supports the Communist Party.'

'So what?'

'The very core of the propaganda of the Student Congress is that we supported the English during the war.'

'The Englishman did not see all the people as different factions – the Soviet Union group, the labourers' group, the mass, etc. When did this dictatorship war became a people's war? Only when Hitler attacked Russia, right? Isn't it your duty to explain it all to the students?' said Manali.

'The Hitler–Stalin pact was made as soon as Poland fell. The question asked often is was Hitler a good man, good enough to make an ally,' said Kesavan.

'The question seems to be yours, not theirs. Russia was the only nation where Socialism was accepted and recognised. All around, capitalist nations were waiting like vultures to devour Russia. Under such circumstances, what could Stalin have done? To save Socialism, to save the people's rule, he had to compromise with Hitler. Was that wrong?' asked Manali.

'Rajaji came out of the Congress and supported the British during the war. What is he doing now? He is an important figure in the group that is having talks with Mountbatten. Does the student congress say Rajaji is a traitor to his country?' asked Somasundaram.

'That's a good point,' said Balan.

'I am not attempting to support the line the student congress has taken. We have to make our standpoint clear in today's meeting,' said Kesavan.

Kesavan began his welcome address as soon as the convention was declared open.

He felt a vacuum in his mind as soon as he began his speech.

Just a few words into the address, and he was all in a sweat.

He noticed that Janaki was in the crowd.

He felt a sudden surge of enthusiasm and words flowed out of him in a torrent.

He spoke against British imperialism; he attacked the world capitalistic tendencies. Then he declared that the Student Congress party was made up of sycophants of the Tatas and Birlas.

Just as he finished speaking, a fair-complexioned man followed by some two or three others came in and sat on the dais.

The crowd broke out into loud cheers of, 'Long live Comrade Mohan.'

10

While the delegates were getting ready for lunch after the morning session got over, Janaki came towards Kesavan with another young man.

Kesavan had already been introduced to that young man and knew him as Jayachandran, a student studying in Chennai. His behaviour and the facility with which he spoke English made him stand apart from other students.

'This is my cousin, Jayachandran, this is Kesavan. You spoke well,' said Janaki

'Thank you. Nice meeting you, comrade,' Kesavan shook Jayachandran's hand.

There was a faint sense of discomfort at the bottom of his mind. He was not going into analysing its nature or what caused it, though.

'Jay is a powerful speaker in English,' said Janaki. The pride in her voice was quite evident.

'What a pity! No one here except Mohan is allowed to speak in English. Come to that, even Comrade Balan can speak admirably well in English, he has been acclaimed by the great Sastri. But Balan will be speaking in Tamil. He is a powerful speaker in Tamil as well,' said Kesavan.

'Yes, yes, I know,' said Jayachandran.

'Why don't you speak in the afternoon session?' suggested Kesavan

'I'm sorry; I'm not all that good in Tamil,' said Jayachandran.

'I didn't expect you to be so good at Tamil,' said Janaki to Kesavan.

'It came as a discovery to me as well. I am sure your cousin can do it if he tried.'

'Why don't you give it a try, Jay?' asked Janaki

'Oh! No! No!' Jay shook his head vehemently.

'Right then, I'm taking Jay home for lunch,' said Janaki

'I don't think that is right; we want all the comrades to sit and have lunch together. You must also eat with us,' said Kesavan.

'My mother has asked Jay to come over for lunch. Moreover, your contention that you comrades are all going to lunch together will not hold any water; Mohan is coming to our house for lunch. Mohan and my brother were classmates in London.

Kesavan stood silent.

'Does it make it okay for us to go home, now?' asked Janaki.

'What say do I have in the matter? Do whatever pleases you.'

After they had gone Kesavan asked Murugesan's brother, 'Is Mohan not having lunch with us here?'

'No, one of his classmates is here in Extension. So he goes there,' said Somasundaram.

'So, that's it?' asked Kesavan.

'Yes.'

Balan who was standing nearby said, 'You should have insisted that we all eat together. That would have made our students happy. Yes?'

Somasundaram moved away without replying to that question.

Kesavan went and sat on one of the chairs in the pandal.

The joy he had felt when he saw Janaki attend the conference was all gone now.

He did not appreciate Mohan going away without sitting down for a meal with all those labour unionists who had so enthusiastically welcomed him.

That all others, except Balan, had accepted Mohan's decision without any demur surprised Kesavan. Children were playing around the posts in the pandal. No evidence of any future student–labour revolution was to be seen there.

He had been planning to ask Mohan many questions; but that gentleman had just smiled, patted him on his back and gone away in Janaki's car. The entire world appeared to be empty and meaningless.

It was no wonder that Janaki had a crush on Jayachandran. He was from the city; he spoke English with consummate ease. His looks were also impressive.

Kesavan came out of the pandal. He did not want to eat there.

If he went home, he would have to eat the ritual meal; if Thatha was really at their house, he would have been happy to see his grandson there.

Kesavan, however never could relish the special kind of food, cooked during those ceremonies.

Amma had earlier mentioned that Thatha was not all that orthodox like Appa. It seems the old man had indulged in many things that were taboo to Vaishanvite Brahmins.

The Sannidi Street legends spoke of his paying early morning visits to Panchami Iyer's hotel to enjoy idlis dipped in onion sambar.

Thatha would be denied onion sambar today; he could not understand how that man's soul was expected to be appeased without getting what he liked to eat.

If Thatha's soul was to be made happy, he must eat onion sambar that day.

He woud not be able to eat it at home that day, not on any other day as well. His father was that strict about it.

He went into Ganapathi Vilas that was just opposite Gandhi Park. He was inwardly shivering with fear that one of Appa's acquaintances might spot him.

At the entrance to Ganapathi Vilas hotel, Thalayatti was buying snuff from a shop that sold snuff.

'What is this Aiyare! You keep on buying snuff on credit; when will you ever settle your account?' the boy at the shop was admonishing Thalayatti.

'Give me just a couple of days more, I'll pay you even if I have to pledge my head. Don't be angry,' Thalayatti was pleading with the shopkeeper.

'Don't pledge your head, your nose should do,' said the boy laughing. Kesavan did not want to sit in the enclosure specified for Brahmins. There may be some familiar face in there.

He sat in the common hall. The eldest son of the owner of the hotel came up to him. That man would have been about forty years old, decked with diamond ear-studs, gold buttons on his shirt, a gold watch chain, another chain around his neck, diamond rings on his fingers...he was always referred to, by the name, '*Minor*'– dandy. They also cited reasons for his eyes being red all the time.

'Aren't you Nadathur Iyengar's son? Why are you sitting here?' asked Minor.

'It is all right.'

'A ceremony in your house?'

Kesavan was taken aback. How did this man know about it? Kesavan did not reply.

'Looks like Chakravarthi Iyengar is one of the special invitees at your house today. He came here this morning to have a cup of coffee. Don't go and tell your father that Chakravarthi Iyengar came there to have the ritual meal, after he had had coffee here,' he laughed as he said these words, and after a short pause, 'but how would you talk about Iyengar to your father, when you are here for a meal? So, tell me what do you want to have?'

'A regular meal.'

'You don't like the meal cooked for a ceremony?'

'No, I don't.'

'Look here, Thambi, you are a Brahmin boy, very daring, perhaps. I cannot even imagine doing what you are doing now. I go to the races, I drink, I consort with prostitutes, but I will not disobey the conventions of my community like you. If ever my father saw me coming to a hotel on the day of a death anniversary ceremony, I would be thrashed black and blue. Anyway, tell me, what do you want to eat, a full meal it is, right?' said the Minor.

'I shall go home and eat,' said Kesavan and got up to leave.

'That would be the best thing to do. The elders will be happy. It is only because Brahmins discard all their prescribed rules of conduct that the other communities do not respect them any more. Now, see what this Chakravarthi Iyengar has done! He has coffee here before he goes for a ceremony in your house. He is a good friend of mine, a master when it comes to giving me race tips. But if he does something wrong, that has to be condemned, yes?'

Kesavan came out of Ganapathi Vilas.

He felt as if 'Minor' had come to save him from doing something wrong.

When he got home, the Brahmins had eaten and were sitting on the *thinnai* chewing betel leaf and nut. They gave Kesavan a smile.

Chakravarthi Iyengar rolled a wad of tobacco and tucked it into his mouth.

'What job was so important that you had to go away? Should you not have stayed at home to receive your grandfather?' asked Chakravarthi.

Kesavan's father came out of the house. He glared at his son for a few seconds.

'I was just asking him where he had been,' said Chakravarthi.

Appa was silent.

'You should not hurt the feelings of elders like this. How nice it would have been if you had stayed at home today. The ceremony gets its name, *Shrarddam* only because it has to be done with *Shrardda*, respect and attention to the conventional rules. What will you, modern boys know about all this? I think it is a waste to make the like of you wear the sacred thread at all,' said Chakravarthi.

Kesavan looked at his father as he spoke, 'You are talking about Brahmin boys, but what about Brahmin elders wearing the sacred thread?' said Kesavan.

'What are you trying to imply?' asked Appa angrily.

'Ask Mama. He had coffee at Ganapathi Vilas this morning before he came here. He gives race tips to Minor. What kind of a Brahmin is he, how better than I am?' said Kesavan.

'All false accusations! Blasphemy!' cried out Chakravarthi.

'Stop all these outbursts. I'll then have to bring Minor here to bear me out.'

Kesavan's father looked at Chakravarthi angrily.

'Don't you believe what this boy is saying,' pleaded Chakravarthi.

'The one important thing that I have learnt from my father is to never utter a lie. I saw Minor of Ganapathi Vilas just a few minutes ago. He told me that you were there at the hotel this morning to have your coffee. I have lost faith in all these conventional practices, only because Brahmins like you deceive the world at large, claiming to have faith in all ritualistic rules. At the same time I learnt another lesson today! Hypocrisy seems to be a quality common to people of all communities, people from all walks of life. There are no exceptions to this rule, be they forward or backward. I'll go in and have my meal now.'

11

*W*hen Kesavan went to his college Murugesan who was standing by the bridge turned away.

Kesavan understood that Murugesan was angry with him.

He took a couple of minutes hesitating whether he should approach Murugesan.

He decided to have the issue sorted out.

'Looks like you are angry with me,' said Kesavan

Murugesan did not reply. He stood staring down at the waters of Cauvery. Kesavan was not sure if he was enjoying watching the swirling waters of the river or gazing vacantly at nothing in particular.

Murugesan's face revealed more disappointment than anger.

'I am sorry, Murugesa, I was not happy with what happened yesterday.'

'What were you not happy about?' asked Murugesan angrily.

'Why didn't Mohan have lunch with all of us? You know he went to have it at Janaki's place, don't you?'

'What business is it of yours anyway, where Mohan had his lunch?'

'We call ourselves communists. But we are unable to ignore the fact that Mohan comes from a well-to-do family. You, tell me, you think it was fair? Do you know that Comrade Balan was also not happy about this?'

'The issue is not whether what Mohan did was right or wrong. Considering that you were the president of the reception committee, your running away to have your lunch at your place is something that cannot be excused. I know why you went home.'

'Tell me why!'

'You were really upset about Janaki taking that comrade from Chennai to her house. Don't pretend that Mohan had anything to do with your action.'

'So, you say what Mohan did was right?'

'They were all asking for you yesterday evening. Could I tell them that you had run away? To save the situation, I had to say that you were sick. Come on, make up your mind, who do you think, is more important, Janaki or the Party.'

'Janaki? What has Janaki got to do with all this?'

'That's just what I would like to know.'

'Progressive or otherwise, I don't like people being hypocritical, that's all!'

'And who was the hypocrite?'

'When you claim that all are equal, shouldn't Mohan have sat with us and had his meal? How happy it would have made the workers!

'Did you do that?'

'Mohan did not and so I too, did not stay.' Murugesan stood there silent, pondering over the issue for a few minutes. Kesavan thought that Murugesan's silence was a sign of the conflict that was going on in his mind about the propriety of Mohan's action.

'My brother is very angry with you. He has said that you should be expelled from the Students' Federation,' said Murugesan, after some time. Kesavan was shocked at this. Murugesan's tone, however, revealed that he was not too keen on executing his brother's command.

Murugesan was a good man; he had a helpful nature. He was very sensitive. Kesavan knew that his friendship with Murugesan was something that went beyond party allegiance.

'Anyway give a written apology that what you did was wrong. I shall try to talk to Annan; The decision will have to be that of the local comrades,' said Murugesan.

Kesavan walked on to the college without giving Murugesan any reply.

Though he heard Murugesan saying after him, 'Hey, what's this? You just go away without saying anything?' Kesavan ignored the call and walked on.

Murugesan ran up to him and shook his shoulder.

'Why will you not apologise? Will that lower your self-esteem?'

'I don't think I have done anything wrong. One should ask forgiveness only if he has done some wrong, yes?'

'What you did was wrong – wrong – without any doubt wrong. You had taken on some responsibility. If you had honoured it and then taken up the issue in the party meeting, others would have understood how your anger was just. But the reason for your sudden desertion was Janaki – that Janaki went home with Jayachandran. I'll say this to you, but not to others. I don't want to hear all this, this silly story about your making a decision to uphold some principle. Just give your apology letter. I have brought back your cycle, take it when you go home,' Murugesan spoke without pausing to take a breath.

Kesavan could not concentrate on his lessons for the rest of the day. Murugesan was, indeed, right.

Why should Janaki's taking Jayachandran home bother him all that much?

How could Janaki be held accountable, if he had infused the stray smiles she dispensed towards him with more than what they might have meant?

He should thank Janaki for kindling his creative powers to find meanings in her smiles.

Subrahmanya Iyer had on many occasions spoken to him of Dante's Beatrice. Kesavan laughed at himself for making bold as to compare himself with Dante. Creative? He?

What a high-sounding word! He had written a story motivated by Janaki's long, beautiful eyes. He had called the story, 'Her Eyes.'

He had seen each line of his story as sheer poetry. But he could not make up his mind as to whom he should read out his story. Murugesan was not interested in literature. Moreover, it was Murugesan's belief that comrades should not be writing love stories.

He was tempted to show the story to Subrahmanya Iyer. Iyer might appreciate him, but he would be teasing him no end.

Kesavan decided to show it to Kovizhiyar. He gave it to Kovizhiyar, saying that it had been written by a relative of his who wanted to know how it read. Kovizhiyar read the story there and then.

Kovizhiyar was quiet for some time. After that he growled aloud, 'Hmm...'

Kesavan was not sure if the professor was clearing his throat or expressing his rating of the story.

Kesavan put out his hand to take back the story.

Kovizhiyar gave it to him without saying anything.

'What do you think of the story?' asked Kesavan.

'So many grammar mistakes, a confusion of singular and plural even if they are acceptable as some that are in vogue, how can one condone mistakes in syntax?' asked Kovizhiyar. Kesavan quietly stood there staring at him.

'Your friend has described his lover's eyes. Does he know how Kamban describes them?'

'What has Kamban said about eyes?'

'Though like lotuses that have come out of shallow water, they are deeper than the mighty ocean. This writer should have quoted Kamban.'

'Quotes are not found in stories. They will then become essays.' said Kesavan.

'You try to teach me how to write a story? I have a hundred stories to my credit.'

Kesavan felt a sudden fear that Kovizhiyar might bring those stories and ask him to read them.

'My stories are all based on literary events. Not like those that claim to be modern literature, those that are a bane on genuine literature. They are stories that uplift mankind – stories that put Mother Tamil on a high throne. Come home, I'll show them to you.'

Kesavan heaved a sigh of relief.

Kesavan wrote many stories after that first, 'Her Eyes', but he did not show them to anyone. He told himself that he was writing for his own satisfaction.

But all his stories had an underlining theme of eyes. Janaki's eyes had had that kind of impact on him.

Janaki was something, her eyes something else. How could there be any connection between those eyes that spoke the innocent language of a child and the Janaki who with English on her lips was attracted by a city-bred young man? Nature had made a mistake. Those eyes did not belong to that face.

Whose face would have suited those eyes better? Kesavan brought up to his mind the faces of many girls he had seen and tried to fit those eyes on them. They did not belong to any of them either. They appeared as cartoons, on any one else.

'You seem to be in some deep thought!'

Kesavan who had been sitting in the library turned around. It was Janaki.

'Lotus eyes like the fathomless sea.' A quote may not have been apt in a short story. But how did that quotation of Kovizhiyar come to his mind then?

How is one ever to translate Shelly's words, 'Baby sleep is pillowed?'

Kesavan stood up.

Janaki smiled. Should those eyes smile too?

'I love you, Janaki' said Kesavan.

12

That laugh of Janaki continued to disturb Kesavan and made sleep elude him....

Some students who were then in the library, looked in their direction. They might have thought that he had said some joke and she had laughed at that.

But was what he told her any joke?

It bothered him that Janaki saw his words as some joke.

'I am sorry, if what I said appears to be funny, forget that I even said it.'

Janaki continued laughing. Kesavan turned his steps out of the library.

'Mr Kesavan, just a minute,' said Janaki.

'Yes, tell me,' Kesavan turned back to face her.

'I thought you were some mature person. You spoke so well at that meeting. Now like any other ordinary boy, you speak words of love.'

'Do you think that speaking out one's mind makes one an average person, ordinary?'

'No! Certainly not! I didn't expect a communist to talk like this, that's all.'

'So it is your opinion that communists do not feel any emotion of love?'

'They may feel it, but they don't give expression to it.'

How is one to declare one's love without speaking about it? Kesavan thought he would ask her the question, but then decided against it.

'Why did you have to laugh so uproariously at what I said?'

'I felt pity for you. You do not have the sort of self-confidence expected of a communist. You have some sort of guilt as if you are doing something wrong.'

So, her objection was only to the manner of his declaring his love! He, again, would have liked to have his doubts confirmed, but refrained from doing it.

She came closer to him and said, 'There is one other thing. I will be marrying my cousin Jayachandran. This is something decided upon a long time ago.'

'I am sorry,' said Kesavan.

'Sorry about what? That I am to marry Jayachandran?'

Kesavan was ashamed of his making a foolish comment for the second time that day. He left the place without saying anything more.

He must have slept only in the early hours of the morning. When he opened his eyes he saw the wall clock showing the time – seven thirty. Amma usually came to wake him if he was in bed after six. Why had she not come?

When Kesavan came down from upstairs, Amma was standing holding on to the pillar, deep in thought.

Appa was in his easy chair. His eyes were closed. Kesavan wondered if he was meditating. But neither Appa nor Amma looked as if they had had their baths. They usually bathe quite early in the morning; why had they not bathed?

He looked at one and then another. Amma signalled him to go, brush his teeth and come back. He went into the yard. When he came back Amma was in the kitchen.

'Your uncle is dead, we have been told,' said Amma.

That uncle was the son of his grandfather's second wife. He had been given away in adoption to Thatha's widowed sister. Very rich initially, but after Chithappa had had his jaunts, what remained were only the clothes on him.

Chithappa would come and sit on the front thinnai, as part of the wall. He would never ask for anything; He would sit there for hours. Kesavan had never seen him talk. Appa had ordained that Chithappa was to be fed whenever he was in the house. He would go away after having a meal and then stay away for days. Suddenly he would show up again.

It was a puzzle where he lived when he was away, where he ate or what he did. He asked his mother once about this and she had said, 'What does it matter where he goes, be happy that he's not here bothering us.'

'What bother is he when he comes here? He does not speak a word. If you feed him he eats, if you don't, he doesn't even ask to be given something to eat,' said Kesavan.

'Praise him all you want. There is not a single prostitute of this town he has not visited. After he has squandered all his wealth, he comes and sits here silently, now. They are supposed to be Brahmins, what can one say of such people!' growled Amma.

'As far as I know all Brahmins except Appa are like this. They have been the reason for the sprouting of a Dravida Kazhagam!' said Kesavan

'That's enough, shut up!'

That uncle was now dead. Kesavan could not make out if Appa was mourning his brother or planning some future course of action.

'Who gave you the news of his death? Where did he die?' asked Kesavan.

'He went to the house, the third house from ours, of Ramaswami Iyengar's 'keep'. He sat there for some time and then just died.'

'Why did he go to that house?'

'This wretched man had had an alliance with the woman's mother. Sometimes he went there to have a meal. They say that this woman was his own daughter.'

'So, Ramaswami Iyengar came here to give you the news?'

'His son Uppili came.'

So, you have to go there now?'

'Some question you ask! The man has died in some low house and you ask if Appa should go there, aren't you ashamed even to ask it?'

'Then why is Appa sitting like this?'

'We cannot have our bath until that man is cremated.'

Ramaswami Iyengar's voice could be heard from outside.

'Mama. Are you coming?'

Kesavan came out of the kitchen. Appa was quiet.

'Say something, Mama. Have we not to find somebody to do the last rites?' asked Ramaswami Iyengar.

Appa's eyes spat fire.

Helpless, Ramaswami Iyengar turned his gaze at Kesavan.

'Has he no children?' asked Kesavan. He really did not know anything about his uncle.

'He never married, come to think of it you are his child.'

'Chee! Shut up!' Appa suddenly raised his voice.

'Now, don't get angry. What was wrong in what I said? Is that man not Kesavan's uncle? Is this boy not entitled to do the rites?'

'Your concubine is the dead man's daughter. Go, ask her to do everything.'

'If our *Shastras* will allow women to do the rites, we can certainly ask her to perform them. But our Shastras do not sanction that.'

'Some Shastra you talk about! You, of all persons, talking of Shastras? You do your service at the Hanuman temple and you are associated with this prostitute. You think, God will accept that?'

'Mama! I am not the issue here. Your brother has chosen to die in that house. He has to be cremated. Now, suggest some way, it can be done.'

13

$\mathcal{K}$esavan was very proud of his father. That Appa cared a hoot for the community's murmurs made him reassess his father.

Appa was orthodox, no doubt. He never missed any of the prescribed rituals. But, that he was clear about not letting those very rituals come in the way of his being a good human being, made Kesavan be proud of his father.

There was a lot of opposition to bringing the dead body to their Sannidhi Street.

Appa did not pay any heed to that.

'That Nadathur Brahmin has lost his senses,' commented the temple priest. They asked Appa, 'Is it fair to bring a dead body into this temple street and starve the God?'

'Even if it is the corpse of some orphan, doing his last rites is equal to doing a *Yagnya*,' said Appa.

They could not do anything against Appa's unrelenting stand and Appa's wealth.

Appa was prepared to spend any amount of money to do the atonement rites as well.

Amma was also not happy with what Appa was doing. But she knew that her opposition had its boundaries which could not be crossed. With just the words, 'some drama the whole thing is!' she had to put an end to her protests.

It all appeared to be a real drama, his uncle's cremation rites. When that man's body was laid in the hall of his house, it was discovered that there was no poonool on that man. Kesavan thought he remembered seeing the poonool on Chithappa whenever he visited their house.

Perhaps the man was in the habit of donning the sacred thread off and on, as and when it suited him, thought Kesavan.

'This is sacrilege; there is no poonool on this man's body,' said Sundaram Vadhyar.

'A poonool should be on him before we get on with the rites,' said Chakkai.

'Making a corpse wear a poonool, what nonsense!' said Appa.

'You have decided to give him a proper farewell. He belongs to the Nadathur clan, he'll go to Vaikuntam only if he departs with the poonool on,' said Chakkai.

'No poonool,' Appa was firm.

'So you want this body to depart this world without belonging to any particular caste, is that it?' asked Sundaram Vadhyar.

Kesavan considered for a moment asking if dead bodies had also caste differences. But he knew Appa would not appreciate the query, so he decided against it.

Appa insisted that Kesavan should perform the rites.

Amma was not for it.

'He is the son who has to do the rites for us. Does it look nice to have him do it for some casteless man?' said Amma.

'I know what is right and what is wrong, you keep your mouth shut,' said Appa.

All the rites that followed did look like a huge circus.

Chithappa was the silent hero of the act. Kesavan thought a faint smile hovered around the dead man's face. He even felt that, perhaps, the man was enjoying the whole *tamasha*.

Some protested against letting Ramaswami's 'keep' from entering the Sannidhi Street.

But Appa not only allowed her to come there, but also let her stay there till the end.

'It is her father. What justice is there, in not allowing her to be present at the rites?' thundered Appa.

'Concubines to enter our houses!' objected Chakkai.

'Ramaswami should be flogged for all this. Why fault her?' said Appa.

'A concubine will always be that, no?'

'Chakkai, don't go on talking. I know the worth of each one of you here. I don't want any more useless talk,' said Appa.

Ramaswami Iyengar's 'keep' looked quite pretty, Kesavan thought. She had Chithappa's sharp nose. She had a big *pottu* on her broad forehead.

Her mother, might have swindled Chithappa of a fortune. But the daughter seemed to be atoning for that sin by helping another Brahmin, that too a poor man.

Of all those present there, she seemed to be the only one shedding tears for the dead man.

Ramaswami Iyengar's wife kept up her abuses of the other woman. But that did not seem to bother her. She stood there silent, until the end, with just a tear-screen veiling her eyes.

Kesavan was not ashamed to go after the bier now as he had been when he was asked to go to the banks of Cauvery on Avani Avittam day.

He was feeling a surge of joy that comes with doing a good deed. He was now prepared to face any number of Peter Rajamanickams now.

But not a familiar face was in sight.

This was a sort of disappointment to him. He had lost the opportunity to boast about his father's large-heartedness.

He did all the rituals of the thirteen days with utmost involvement. He had never before obeyed his father's commands so happily.

He saw Appa in a new light now.

A new hero.

A hero so human that he cared for all his fellow human beings.

Appa might have had a deep faith in the customs and rituals that his caste prescribed, but it was clear that he hated the hypocrisy he saw all around him.

He did not, however, react to this negatively by giving up his customs.

Subrahmanya Iyer was one who had given up all caste rites and rituals in protest against this kind of hypocrisy.

Kesavan posed this question to himself, 'what would he end up becoming?'

Come to think of it was there anybody who was not play acting?

Were the progressive thinkers free of this? Had he not seen their true faces in the recent student conference?

While his mind was grappling with such questions even as he was trying to concentrate on the trigonometry book that he had in his hand, Appa's voice could be heard loud and clear.

'Who wants your money? How dare you come into my house and offer me this money?'

Kesavan went downstairs.

Ramaswamy Iyengar's 'keep' was standing in front of his father.

She gave Kesavan a smile.

'You must excuse me, you should not be angry with me. This money had been left with me by your brother for his last rites. This is not my money, I promise you, this is not mine at all!'

'How am I to believe that he had left this money with you?' asked Appa.

'You have to take my word for that. He was particular that his ceremonies should be done with his money and so had deposited the amount with me. It is not a lie; I promise you.'

'Why did you not say anything about this earlier?'

She did not reply.

'Come on. Tell me why did you not disclose this truth then?'

'I was scared that the rites would then get done in my house, Kesavan may not do them. The dead man wanted Kesavan to do them.'

'Did he ever mention that?'

'Yes.'

Appa got up from his easy chair and locking his hands behind him spent the next few minutes in thought.

Amma came out of the kitchen.

'Don't take the money, that will not be right,' she said.

'Don't say that. If you don't take it his soul...'

'Stop it. You dare speak about what is right!' interrupted Amma.

'You know how happy I was that the rites were all performed here? That Periappa made it happen, without any fear of the community...'

'Periappa? Who is that?' asked Amma shocked.

'I am talking about Kesavan's father.'

'Oh, God! So you try to establish kinship, is that it? Some Periappa he is to you, are you not ashamed to claim this?' Amma burst out.

'I am not going to get angry at anything you say. That was my father's wish, I have to fulfil it. I should have handed over this money earlier. I didn't, I am sorry. But I have given you my reasons for not doing that.'

'Right, you give the money to the temple and use it to do the monthly rituals,' said Appa.

'There is money to cover all that, even the death anniversaries...'

'Some paltry sum it must be, how much is it?' asked Amma.

'Twenty thousand rupees.'

Appa was aghast.

'How much did you say it was?'

'Twenty thousand.'

Appa looked at her trying to size her up. He did not expect a woman who had all along been described only as a 'keep' to come to him with so big an amount. This was evident in the look he gave the woman.

'From where did he get that much money?' asked Appa.

'Even my mother was not aware of this. If she had known about it, she would have snatched it away from him. So, he gave it to me only after my mother's death. I haven't mentioned it even to my husband.'

'Your husband! Who is your husband? You usurp another woman's rights and come here to speak of kinship with all of us!' said Amma.

'Will you keep your mouth shut?' said Appa to Amma angrily.

'Why are you angry with me? Some immoral woman comes to our house and gives us money as if she is giving us alms and you are not speaking out against it! Is this proper?' said Amma.

Kesavan had never heard Amma speak to Appa in this manner. Was this anger at the injustice done to another wife? Or had it come out of a self-preservation instinct to protect herself against a woman of no virtue, who may go to any length to ensnare a man? Amma's body was trembling slightly in anger.

'Are you in your right senses? Is this woman characterless, this one who brings some twenty thousand rupees claiming that her father wanted it to be spent on his last rites?

'Half the men of this street are bent on swindling the temple money, spending it on prostitutes. If Ramaswamy goes and falls into her lap, is she to be held responsible for the folly? All right, you, woman, listen, Uppili is also my brother's grandson in a way. You deposit this money in the bank, let it be used to educate that boy.'

14

*A*ugust 15, 1947.

When Kesavan opened his eyes in an Independent India it was eight in the morning.

There was a reason for his sleeping in so late.

There had been a big altercation in Vakil Lakshminarasimha Iyengar's house the previous night.

He could not even listen properly to Nehru's midnight speech.

Screams and shouts came up from the street.

When he came down and out to the entrance, Appa and Amma were standing there.

'What's the uproar about?' he asked Amma.

'It is from the Vakil's house.'

'What happened there?'

Peria Mottai came up to them, stuffing snuff into his nose.

'What is all the ruckus about?' Appa asked

Peria Mottai wiped his nose.

'Affairs in high places,' said Peria Mottai.

'What is it?' asked Appa.

Vakil's family is not there in his house. They have all gone to Mannarkudi. Vakil was alone in the house.' Having said this he laughed loudly.

Kesavan could not understand what there was to laugh about in the Vakil being all by himself in his house.

'Tell me what happened, leave your laughter for later,' Appa said, it was clear he was losing his patience.

'The servant maid of that house, a pretty girl, Kesava, you go inside.'
Kesavan remained there.

'Vakil has tried to act fresh with her. That girl has brought all her people here. Is that it?' asked Appa.

'Yes.'

'And this was the man who stood for the election pleading, "Vote for the yellow box" Look how your leader behaves! said Appa.'

'And that too on Independence day,' drawled Peria Mottai.

'Freedom to do as they please, that is what freedom means to them,' said Appa.

The clamour increased.

'Come out, you Iyere!' was the cry.

Kesavan was surprised that even at the height of their anger they used the term of respect for a Brahmin.

Appa went out of his house.

'Look! Appa is out to dispense justice; he is sure to get beaten, that's it,' said Amma.

'These people are always abusing us, calling us 'Pappaans' derogatively. Should our Mama go there now?' said Peria Mottai.

'Kesava, go with Appa,' said Amma.

Kesavan followed his father.

Appa went near that crowd.

'What's all this shouting?' asked Appa.

'Come here, Iyere! This Iyer tried to molest our girl. So now we want justice. That man stays inside the house, locking himself up in there. If he is really some man, ask him to step outside!' said one from the crowd.

He must have been around twenty. He appeared to be very drunk.

'Look here, I am not saying that what the Vakil did was right. Come in the morning, is it fair that you come here and raise this outcry, spoiling the sleep of all around here?' said Appa.

'By morning the man will be gone,' said another.

'What is it that you want to do now?'

'He must come out accept that what he did was wrong, fall at our feet and ask for forgiveness.'

'Is that all? Tomorrow I'll talk to him and...'even as Appa was speaking, one from the crowd interrupted him. 'We don't want all those stories about tomorrow. The bird will fly away. Ask him to give us some money for our drinks now; we shall drink and celebrate the Independence Day!'

'You ass! Go away! Only because there are drunks like you around, these Brahmins do whatever they want,' said a young man.

'Hey! Why do you have to prick this Aiyar's heart with your barbs, talking about Brahmins and all?' said a middle-aged man. Kesavan was not sure if he was mocking or if he really felt that Appa should not be insulted.

'The young man is right – today's Brahmins, men like this Vakil, sure do whatever they want. It is the same story in every house of this Sannidhi Street. If only Brahmins lived the way they were ordained to, there would not have been any need for all this contention. But if you really want to show that you are people with self-esteem, don't stand on the street and shout like this. Get two of you to stand guard at the back entrance and two at the front. We shall meet again in the morning and sort it all out. What do you say?' asked Appa.

'That's a good idea,' said an elderly man.

'Then, who is to pay for our drinks? Iyere, will you?'

'Shut up!' shouted one.

After some discussion among themselves, they decided to post a couple of men, both at the front and back entrances of the house.

After Appa came back home, Peria Mottai asked, 'Mama! Why did you have to get into this?'

'Look, to put it in their language, all the 'Pappaans' hide inside their houses and just watch the fun. Did anyone go to talk to them? If you have done something wrong, then you'll be scared to speak; I have done no wrong; so I could make bold to go, talk to them. They know to respect and honour this courage of mine,' said Appa.

'What would you have done if they had decided to thrash the "Pappaans" and attacked you?' asked Peria Mottai.

'"Pappaans" sure need to be flogged, especially a "Pappaan" like this Vakil.... He claims he fought for our Independence. Scoundrel! Calls himself a trustee of the temple and swindles the temple money. Has he spared a single prostitute of this town? Didn't you all hear what he has done? A servant maid, just the age of his daughter and he molests her! Why would not all those people decry it as the arrogance of the Pappaans?' Appa spoke angrily, breathing fast.

'Looks like you will join forces with the Dravida Kazhagam, Mama!' said Peria Mottai.

'Ask Kesavan what happened on that ceremony day at our house. A Brahmin, supposed to come pure and fasting to participate in the ceremony goes to Ganapathi Vilas, has his fill of onion sambar and then comes here. What sort of a Brahmin is he?'

'That's enough. It is late, come inside,' said Amma.

Kesavan felt that all Appa's pent up anger was streaming out. Otherwise, he would not have openly subjected Sannidhi Street to such harsh criticism.

After they came in, Appa told Kesavan, 'See this irony! We have just got our independence today. In the name of Satyagraha, he bribed his way into an "A" class prison and look what he has gone and done today! People like him will be our rulers now. Gandhi must have realised the truth and so moved away, deciding to have nothing to do with any of this.'

'No, that was not the reason; Pakistan...' began Kesavan when

Amma interrupted him and said, 'That's enough. Go to sleep. We have had enough of this night-drama.'

Kesavan could not sleep for quite a while. This incident was bothering him. Should it happen right on Independence Day?

Vakil's father was also a vakil, who must have been around 75 years; it was said that he lived in the Extension area with a middle-aged lady. Perhaps this was a genetic trait at work!

He understood his father's anger.

When he came down at eight next morning, his mother told him, 'Brush your teeth, have coffee and go to that house. There's no stopping your father. He's already there.'

When Kesavan went there, police were there. Appa was shouting angrily.

'This is not fair. I told them to post two men at the front and two at the back of this house. To arrest them saying that they were here to rob the house is gross injustice. Laksminarasimha, you are a Brahmin! You should have some conscience. Don't you know that what you are doing is utter roguery?' Vakil sat on a chair saying nothing.

The policemen had two of those deputed to keep watch in their custody. The other two must have fled. Kesavan said, 'I am this gentleman's son. It was Appa who had asked them to stay here last night. They are no thieves.'

Vakil said with a smile playing on his face, 'They jumped into the house and were trying to open the locked cupboard, when I caught them red-handed And your father, a scholar in his own right, an elderly man at that, is accusing me of all kinds of things; is it fair? You appoint yourself a witness and come to speak on behalf of your father. You are a comrade, you belong to the party that was cringing before the whites in 1942. It is now our rule.' Appa intercepted the Vakil and said, 'say it is your rule!'

The police inspector said, 'Periyavare! Will anyone from this street come and bear witness to your claim that things happened the way you say they did?'

'No, they will not, Ask Peria Mottai and he will stand there as if he doesn't know a thing. This is how upright all the people of this street are. A big crowd came with these two accused, perhaps you should ask some of them,' said Appa.

'We have made our enquiries. They also say that nothing like what you say ever happened here.'

'Then, where is that girl?' thundered Appa.

'They say that she has not been in this place for the past two months.' Vakil continued to smile. Kesavan understood that whatever needed to be done had all been accomplished over the telephone.

Appa looked pathetic. He was walking out of that house silently.

Kesavan did not see any difference between Gandhiji's silence and Appa's silence.

The day was August 15, 1947.

15

$\mathcal{K}$esavan was in the playground.

They were all sitting and chatting after a cricket match. Narasimhachari had made 130 runs that day. His playing had led to the team from Tiruchi to lose. Not only had he made a century, he had four wickets to his credit as well.

Narasimhachari, excelling as he did in that white man's game, had not yet sacrificed his tuft. He would have his hair tightly knotted and covered with a turban, when he played. It was a wonder for all who saw him that he could play without the turban coming unwound during the game.

The games-master Pannirselvam had tried any number of times to convince him. 'You play a good game. You may even get a chance to play in the Ranji Trophy tournament. But if you go there, you will be asked to remove your tuft. So, why don't you do it now?'

Yet remove his tuft, he never would, rather never could. After having had fourteen children, his father had taken *sanyas*, and was now the head of some Vaishvanite Mutt.

Narasimhachari was the youngest in his family. His elder brother was old enough to be his father. That brother had occasionally visited Kesavan's house to meet with his father.

His colleagues teased Narasimhachari to his face about his large family.

'Does your mother know all your names?'

'Why not? Does she not have a roll call every morning? How can she forget the names?' Narasimhachari would reply.

Today he had played exceptionally well. He had made 18 boundaries. Kesavan went up to Narasimhachari who was standing on the field surrounded by his fans and shook the hero's hands.

'Thank you,' said Narasimhachari.

He had taken his turban off. The tightly knotted tuft had also been set free; it was quite a sight to see it beautifully swaying in the breeze.

He had on white pants, white shirt; over these came the tuft and the caste mark on his forehead. Seemed like East and West were meeting in a straight line.

'All you eat is insipid cereal and rice and yet you score so highly on the field, how do you ever manage that?' asked Panchavanam.

'Don't forget the cooked rice from the previous day that I have in the morning, in addition to cereals and rice. Cast aside your goat curry and try this menu, you will also get your scores,' said Narasimhachari.

Paanirselvam stood aside with a smile on his face, smoking and enjoying the conversation of the youngsters.

He was a placid man. Not easily given to emotions. When he spoke, it would be deliberate with long pauses in between the words.

Exaggeration was something he was totally ignorant of.

Robert had reported what the master had told Narasimhachari after he had made the century. He had shaken his disciple's hand and said, 'Not bad, you...played, fairly well...'

Pannirselvam stood there listening to these comments as well, with just a smile on his face.

Robert then looked at Kesavan and called out, 'Kesava, come here. Make this fellow cut off his tuft. Remember, we had been to Madurai last month for a game? He had not secured his turban properly and the tuft was also not tied properly. He ran and what a sight he was then, loose hair and all!'

'Perhaps if the tuft comes off, he may not play this well. Maybe all his skill lies in his hair like Samson's did...' Before Kesavan could finish his sentence, Panchavanam intervened and said, 'If he is some Samson, what Delilah would come attracted by his tuft?'

'If one such Delilah comes and orders the tuft be removed, off will it go, never mind cricket or tradition,' quipped Robert.

'You should not be talking in this way,' said Pannirselvam. That was the limit of his anger. The general rule was that games masters were ominous and feared by the students. Perhaps the rule applied to schools, not colleges.

A student came running to them, quite out of breath.

'Sir! Sir! Sir!' was all he could say.

'Yes, tell us what happened,' said Robert his hand firmly on the boy's shoulder.

'It is...Mahatma Gandhi has been shot!'

'What!?' all their voices rose in unison.

'Yes, they say, he was shot as he was coming for the prayer meeting.'

Pannirselvam calmly came up with just this comment. 'Mahatma Gandhi was a good man.'

This understatement, so out of tune with the emotional state they were all in, irritated Kesavan.

He left the place.

Why did Gandhi's death affect Kesavan all that much? He had not appreciated all the stands that the leader had taken.

The one about linking religion with politics – and the symbolic struggle he advocated; can just making thread on a charkha bring independence to the country, he had always wondered?-

It was Kesavan's opinion that Independence, that should have been theirs, as a matter of course, much earlier, had been delayed only because of Gandhi.

'Just because people burnt a police station, he opted out of the movement, didn't he! If he had let things take their course, considering the collective opinions of the people, independence would have been theirs then!' – Kesavan had felt that this criticism of Gandhi by Rajani Palme Dutt was a fair one.

And yet, the courage of conviction and the personal valour the man had exhibited during the recent riots had created waves in Kesavan's mind.

Who else could have made the Navakali trip? Who else could have gone on a fast, even though the man was in agony about the partition of Pakistan, insisting that 56 crores of rupees that justly belonged to the new country should be paid to it in full? Who else could have insisted that all the refugees who had taken shelter in the mosques of Delhi be removed from there and be put up in camps erected specially for them?

The news of a bomb being flung at the leader some ten days ago at a prayer meeting should have alerted the police. However Gandhi had refused to have any police protection. The kind of faith he had in his people!

Just six months after the country had become free, the country's first human sacrifice had been made! And it was by taking the life of the Father of the Nation!

Kesavan felt strong emotions tug at his heart. Unawares to him, Gandhiji seemed to have penetrated his consciousness.

He felt like crying; with difficulty he controlled himself.

He was surprised that Gandhiji had made such a deep impression on him.

When his mother's father had died the previous year, he had not cried. He had thought that he loved that grandfather very much. He tried to remember all the love and concern the old man had shown him and yet he had not shed any tears then.

But Gandhiji was not even aware of his existence. And, yet his death churned Kesavan's insides. This was a personal loss to him; a loss that nothing ever could make up for.

He had once seen Gandhiji, from quite a distance when he was at school.

People jostled each other at the banks of Arasalaru. Gandhiji had greeted them with folded hands, standing at the doorway of the compartment of the train he was travelling by.

Gandhiji did not speak that day; it was his day of silence.

Kesavan had then wondered how was it that the entire country, Bharath stood mesmerised by this half-clad old man?

That meeting had not made any significant impact on him.

A man who dared to speak only the truth had been killed. An ideal man who would not sacrifice truth just to please the people, had been shot at.

Would any other political leader have dared to make enemies of the people?

But Gandhi was no man of politics.

Patel was a politician; he had argued that the 56 crores due to Pakistan be used for the rehabilitation of the refugees who had fled Pakistan to come to India. But no one ran to Pakistan as a refugee. They either went out of their own choice or because they were afraid of their safety.

But the Muslims in India had the confidence that as long as Gandhi was alive, they would be safe.

That was the greatness of the man!

He had been killed!

When he got back home, Appa was listening to the radio.

Mourning tunes.

He sat by his father's side.

'There was one good man around; now he's gone as well,' said Appa.

'Nehru is also a good man,' said Kesavan. Appa did not pay any heed.

'How cruel! The rogue has shot the leader!' lamented Appa.

'Who is the culprit?'

'Some Godse they said his name was. They also suspect that he belonged to RSS. What party is this RSS? '

'It is not any party, it is a movement. A movement that seeks to restore the Hindus to their ancient glory, a revival of a golden age, as it were.'

'So that is why they have gone and shot another Hindu?'

'Many Hindus did not like Gandhiji insisting that the 56 crores be paid to Pakistan.

'This is no Hindu-Muslim issue. It is about honouring a promise. The one thing that Hindu religion harps on time and again is Truth; believes that truth will win – *Satyameva Jayate*. What had been promised cannot under any circumstance be not given, whatever reasons you may come up with. That is definitely unacceptable. Look at the freedom you have got! The first to be sacrificed is the man who got you the freedom!' said Appa.

Kesavan could understand the impact Gandhi had made on Appa too.

Amma was in the kitchen.

'I don't want to eat Amma. I'm not hungry,' said Kesavan.

'Why? Because Gandhi has been shot?'

'It is not just that. I am not hungry. Maybe that is also a reason.'

'Good man he was! One look at him and you would be convinced of his goodness. How could one have the heart to shoot such a gentle person?'

Gandhiji had touched Amma as well. He had touched each one of his country to some measure.

Appa could be heard shouting at someone outside.

'Go see, who he is shouting at, his anger seems to be on the rise nowadays,' said Amma.

Chakkai was standing in the hall.

Appa was speaking in a loud voice.

'What kind of a man are you that you can say that it is good that Gandhi died? No killing can ever be justified. It is a sin. That is our *Dharma*. You say that he had gifted away our country to the Muslims!

What did he give away? Who do you buy your greens from – who do you buy your betel leaves from? The other day you ran with your grandson to Melakaveri, crying that some poisonous insect or snake had bitten him, who did you run to then? How did any Muslim harm you? It is all this politics that has cropped up to create divisions among people who lived happily together. Only God can save the country now!'

16

Kesavan was walking along the Gandhi Park. People stood in groups, talking. Kesavan thought that grief was written on all their faces.

It was at this very Gandhi Park that guns had been fired during the 1942 August meeting. He had been a schoolboy then. It was fun to watch whatever was happening there. When the police started to fire, the crowd ran helter-skelter with shouts of Mahatma Gandhi ki Jay! and Vande Mataram!

Mahatma Gandhi's name had become a magic word. He remembered how he had run into the lane by the park and got home through the backyard of another house that had its front in Sannidhi Street.

He could hear the sound of gun shots; and also the cries of the crowd, Mahatma Gandhi ki Jai!

He thought of that incident now. The Hotels were all closed. But the radios were relaying Gandhi's favourite song, 'Vaishnava Janato'.

Just a few days ago he had read in a magazine the meaning of the lyrics of 'Vaishnava Janato'.

He could also recollect how at that time he had thought – what kind of a song is this, listing out the ethical and moral qualities a man should have. Why is Gandhiji making a religious ritual of politics?

Yet now, the song seemed to have a new dimension, a sort of sadness that tugged at his heart strings. It was not the song, but the way it was sung that, perhaps, created the melancholy mood; that it was the great man's favourite and was being broadcast under such sorrowful circumstances – all these together had combined to make his eyes wet.

He was a little ashamed at his being carried away so easily by emotions.

All the shops were also closed. He remembered what Nehru had said the previous evening, 'The light is gone – not gone by itself – it has been snuffed out.'

Who exactly was this man Godse? How angry he must have been with Gandhi if he had decided to kill Gandhi, shooting him straight from the front!

He had some knowledge of RSS party. This man, Kranthikar, had approached him on many occasions and asked him to join their combat practices. Not once had that gentleman talked to him any politics. Murugesan had spoken to him of Kranthikar, 'these people want the Hindus to rule the country; they want all the Muslims to be driven away from this land.'

When Kesavan had asked, 'Why should the Muslims be driven away?' Murugesan had replied, 'That's, exactly, the point, that's why our party opposes them.'

There was a permanent calm on Kranthikar's face. He could not even imagine that the man would harm anybody, let alone drive away the Muslims.

'Combat practices' were some kind of drill. Another friend of his, Rangaswami used to attend the physical exercise classes that RSS conducted. He looked odd in his khaki shorts and white shirt, Kesavan thought.

Rangaswami was very much interested in history. He would always be talking about Shivaji. It was this obsession with Shivaji that had drawn him to Kranthikar and he had joined the RSS movement.

Kesavan went to Sayabu's 'betel leaf – areca nut' shop that was in Melakaveri. That was the regular haunt of his friends.

Sayabu had not been in favour of a separate Pakistan. He kept up his abuses of Jinnah all the time.

'He does not offer any *namaz*, cannot speak Urdu, who is he to dictate orders to us?' Sayabu would fume.

If he was asked, 'Sayabu, do you know Urdu?' he would say, 'Why should I know Urdu. Jinnah lives in the north. His mother tongue is Urdu. Shouldn't one know his mother tongue? My mother tongue is Tamil.'

'Jinnah is not from North India, he lives in Bombay, he should know Gujarati.'

'Be it so, but they say he knows only English. Shouldn't he be familiar with Gujarati?'

'Sayabu, don't you want to go to Pakistan?'

'I don't want to go to any cussed place. Stop all this loose talk, tell me what you want, betel combo or cigarette?'

When Kesavan went to Sayabu's shop, though the shop was closed Sayabu was sitting outside on a stool. His face was drawn. He was smoking a beedi.

Sayabu got up when he saw Kesavan.

'Sit down, Thambi.'

'Don't get up, you sit down.'

'He has killed a great man, heartless sinner that he is!' said Sayabu.

Kesavan asked, 'Can I have a cigarette?'

'I'll not open the shop. But you can have a draw at this beedi, here take it.'

'Did Murugesan come here?' asked Kesavan.

'There he is, I can see him coming,' said Sayabu as he looked in the opposite direction.

Murugesan was not alone. Four others, Chinnayyan, Anvar, Gopu and Venkataraman were also with him.

As soon as they neared him, Murugesan told Kesavan, 'Comrade, we are holding a protest meeting this evening, against caste system, this country will see progress only if we get rid of all these Hindu Maha Sabah people.'

'A protest meeting? Let us keep our protest for a later day. We need to first have a condolence meeting. Just when the entire nation is in tears...' before Kesavan could finish his sentence, Venkataraman interrupted him, 'You have to strike the iron while it is hot; only if you have a protest meeting and talk to them of the evils of caste now, it will reach the people.'

'Should we not express our sorrow at Gandhi's death? Isn't that more important? Let us not start crying out slogans, let's start with having a silent procession,' said Kesavan

'No one understands silence, only raised voices will appeal to them,' said Chinnayyan.

'No one now is in a state to take in any propaganda. They are all in a state of shock,' said Kesavan

Sayabu said, 'Why, Thambi, all these protests? Will people shed tears in a house that has seen a death or will they be having meetings? Have your meetings and all such things later on.'

'Sayabu, you know nothing of politics, just keep quiet!' said Murugesan.

'A great man is dead. Where is any politics in this?' asked Sayabu.

'He did not just die, he was shot dead. We have to break the power that is behind this man who shot Gandhiji,' said Chinnayyan.

'We sure did call Gandhi a non progressive man. We don't deny it. But we never denied that he was a good man,' said Murugesan.

'I know all about this, Thambi. Though I am only a small-time shopkeeper, I am well aware of all that goes on around me. Were you any part of the August revolution? You ran behind the whites then,' said Sayabu.

'We never were for any whites, Sayabu. The Russians entered the fray, Russia is the land of workers. The common enemy was Hitler.

You will not understand all these complex issues, Sayabu! Sweets were distributed at the news of Gandhi's assassination,' said Chinnayyan.

'Some rumours they all are. When each one is grieving over it as if it is a personal sorrow, will anybody be so bold as to distribute sweets?' asked Murugesan.

'It is your problem if you will not believe this,' retorted Chinnayyan angrily.

'They say that sweets were distributed in Poona,' said Kesavan.

'Some sycophants of the British in our town may have done it, aren't there so many Rao Sahibs and the like around us, here?'

'You are wrong, all those British title-holders will now become Congress Party members,' said Murugesan

'They are already in the Congress,' said Venkataraman.

'They will start wearing Gandhi caps instead of hats,' said Chinnayyan.

'That is exactly why I feel, our people have to be tutored to go the right way,' said Murugesan.

Subrahmanya Iyer always said, 'If and when we get freedom, the browns instead of the whites will rule the country. The marginalised sections of the society will remain very much where they are.' 'I should go see him, now. It has been days since I saw him,' said Kesavan

'All we need is another revolution to set things right,' said Venkatraman.

'What kind of revolution?' asked Kesavan.

'A Communist revolution, an agricultural revolution. A revolution to drive away Vadapthimangalam, Kunniyur and the like,' said Murugesan raising his voice.

17

When Kesavan went to Subrahmanya Iyer's house he was reclining in an easy chair in the yard, deeply engrossed in a book. When he saw Kesavan he said, 'Come in, Kesavan! It is quite sometime since I saw you.'

'Every time I set out to visit you something or other crops up to make me put off my visit,' said Kesavan

When he sat on the ground in front of Iyer and rested his back on the wooden pillar, sawdust fell off the pillar.

'It seems to be crumbling,' said Kesavan as he gave the pillar a shake.

'Isn't it also ageing like me? Come to think of it, it is fifty years older. The house was built by my grandfather,' said Iyer. 'Let the pillar be! You tell me how is college? After I retired from service not a single living being comes to see me. You were visiting me now and then, but you have also become so big and busy that you don't have the time for it,' Iyer went on.

'No, Sir! Some big and busy man I will never become! Everything is happening just as you said it would. The only difference is the skin colour, brown instead of white, that's all! Police resorted to shooting in Mannarkudi the day before yesterday! And that too because the farm workers wanted more wages!' said Kesavan. Subrahmanya Iyer was rubbing his knees with a smile on his face.

'The landlords were all part of the Justice Party until yesterday and today they are all with the Congress!' Kesavan's voice sounded a little high.

'What do you expect them to do?' asked Iyer.

'I don't understand how the Congress has allowed them to come in.'

'What is it that you don't understand? You said they were landlords – the white rulers have left – now these Congressmen have to contest the elections. Don't they need money for that? Will your farmhands be able to provide the money?'

'A constitution has been drawn up. According to this constitution, all above the age of 21 will have the right to vote. Come January 26, India will become a Republic. Will not all these leaders come begging for votes from these same farm hands?' asked Kesavan. Iyer laughed.

'Now, what makes you laugh?'

'Is the horse before the cart or the cart before the horse?'

'I don't understand you.'

'In this country with its 7% literacy, what has happened is that before making an attempt to educate them, they have been handed the right to vote! Isn't this like putting the cart before the horse?'

'Everyone has the right to education,' said Kesavan.

'If the country can afford it and it makes education free and compulsory for all those under sixteen, only then, will our experiment with democracy succeed. If that is not done, those with money or their *benaami* owners will rule the country.'

'Going by the constitution,' began Kesavan when Iyer intervened, 'Look here; the constitution is just a piece of paper. Is it enough if it defines what is right and what is wrong? We have to make an effort to bring them into practice. Untouchability is totally unacceptable. OK, we have a law against it. But isn't the scavenger woman in your house entering your house only through the backyard? The Harijans should be allowed inside the temples. Our law says so. OK. Yet it is beyond me why they should even want to go to the temples. Will that take care of their hunger? Your Communist Party pays no attention to all these issues and it is funny that it is busy organising protests claiming – that wages of eight annas is not enough and that it should be raised to one rupee!.'

'If there is economic progress...'

Kesavan tried to reason when Iyer went on, 'When will you have economic progress? Only when you know what your rights are, yes? When will that happen? Only when they are educated enough to question and understand everything. Right? So our first priority should be to make Primary and High school education compulsory for all. But I know, these politicians will not want that. If the people are all educated, they will not be able to swindle them. Anyway, all this is just empty talk. Tell me, how is your father?' said Iyer.

'Didn't I tell you once? My father is not as conservative as he appears to be.'

'What is being conservative?'

'Holding to all ancient beliefs. A kind of backwardness that makes one live in an earlier age, perhaps centuries earlier, believing that the value system of those years are to be followed forever,' said Kesavan.

Iyer clapped his hands.

'You have all the makings of a politician,' Iyer said.

'You are making fun of me,' said Kesavan

'No, my boy – this is appreciation. Go ask your father about this. He will not bother about all these conservatisms and progressivisms. He goes about saying what he thinks is right. A good man is a progressive man, did you know that?'

'I have been admitted as a party member,' said Kesavan.

'Very good, great!'

'Yes sir, it is something great. It is not all that easy to become a member of the Communist Party. There was a lot of opposition from the locals that I should not be made a member. They said that I had a lot of bourgeoisie tendencies within me. But it was the strong lobbying of Murugesan that has helped me get in,' said Kesavan.

'Communism is, indeed, a great concept. There is no doubt about it whatsoever. But what I don't like is the Communist party having Russia as a model to follow. When an intellectual idea is put into practice, it somehow becomes diluted, making a mockery of the concept.' said Iyer.

'How so?' asked Kesavan

'Not just Marxism, Advaita and Buddhism also have fallen into this trap.'

'Is Marxism a religion?'

'Wherever there are rituals, that system becomes a religion.' said Iyer.

'Which do you say are rituals?'

'Mouthing clichés! Just like our priests chant the mantras, all the communists go around mouthing the same clichés.'

'What if they are clichés? The Communist Party is the only party today that supports the causes of the poor. Dravida Kazhagam is bent on punishing me for all the aberrations of my grandfathers. They don't seem to have any economic agenda.'

'What sort of economic plans does your party have?'

'Socialism.'

'How do you plan to bring that about?'

'Revolution.'

'Rebel for small causes; one rupee and two rupee causes? Mao Se Tung is very much in the forefront in China; in no time you'll see him drive Chiang Ke Shaik away. Can you think of any protest that your party might consider for a large vision?'

'China is not the same as India.'

'They are the same. I tell you today, Mao will not run behind Russia – that is for sure. Do you have a leader like him?'

'Our problem today is not about party leadership. Political revolution should be followed by economic revolution. My contention is that only the Communist Party will be able to bring about this revolution. That's why...' Kesavan had not completed the sentence when Iyer raised his palm to stop him.

'Please, I do not say you are wrong in joining this party. It is only fair that you do what you think is right. There is no need for you to tow my line of thought. Maybe, I would have also felt like you when I was your age. I do not belong to your generation now. But I am sure of this; letting the poor stay poor would be to the advantage of the politicians. If there is no poverty, the parties will have no slogan to shout aloud!'

'In Russia, they did away with poverty and yet the party is as influential as ever before,' said Kesavan.

'I don't know if poverty has been eradicated in Russia or not. I have never gone beyond Kumbakonam. But I feel that poverty is not about only hunger for food. If there is no freedom to think or write as it pleases one, then that would mean poverty of sorts as well, a kind of cultural poverty...Arthur Koestler, Stephen Spender...they were all influenced by Communism at one point in their lives. But now...'

Kesavan did not let Iyer finish his sentence. 'But they are all sycophants of the USA.'

Iyer smiled.

'What does your smile mean?'

This war has divided the world into two, The American world and the Russian world.

Each nation's foreign policy will now be about which side they are going to be on. Our Nehru is a Fabian Socialist. So, Russia will be our friends for now.'

'Anything wrong with that?' asked Kesavan.

'Nothing at all,' said Iyer in a teasing tone.

18

'*K*esava!'

The harshness in Appa's voice surprised Kesavan.

He came down.

The Sanskrit professor, Panchapakesa Sastrigal was sitting there with Appa.

It was two years since Sastrigal retired from Kumbakonam College. Sanskrit bound Appa to him.

'What is your course of study in MA?' asked Appa.

Kesavan had been admitted into the postgraduate course of the Annamalai University. There was no vacancy in the hostel; so he had come back home. Today he was going back to Chidambaram; he intended to meet with the Vice Chancellor and somehow get a room in the Hostel.

'Tamil,' said Kesavan.

'Tamil?'

'Didn't I tell you it was Tamil? Kovizhi told me, 'Sastrigale! Times are changing. A Brahmin boy goes to study Tamil MA. And the boy is your friend's son. Kesavan.' I didn't understand why he has done it.

Kesavan is very good at English; but he chooses to study Tamil, not English, why?' Sastrigal went on.

'Sir, you are a Sanskrit teacher and yet you would like me to study English? What is wrong in my going in for Tamil? That is why the Dravida Kazhagam people say we are Aryans...' said Kesavan.

'Will they accept you in their fold, say, you are a Dravidian, if you study Tamil?' countered Sastrigal.

'I am not looking for anybody's approval or sanction. I like Tamil, so I want to study it.'

'Already they are out to rout the Tamilians. What sort of a job do you hope to get with your Tamil degree? Just because you have opted to study Tamil no one is going to praise you or honour you, put you on a pedestal. Remember that whatever you do, you will remain a Brahmin.,' said Sastriyar angrily.

'I was hoping that you would attempt the civil services exam, IAS. If you study Tamil, will you be able to appear for those exams?' asked Appa.

'IAS exams and the like, need a special kind of skill to pass them – I know I don't have it,' said Kesavan

'What skills are you talking about? Remember Veerasami Iyengar who would forever be seen lying with his legs thrown over one another, on the wall in Pachai Mudali street? His son could be heard early morning croaking like a frog, getting his lessons by heart. He has now passed the IAS and you say you can't?' said Sastrigal

'That is exactly the skill I am talking about. I don't have it. I don't intend joining some government office either,' said Kesavan.

'What is it then that you intend to do? If becoming a teacher is to be your fate, who can help you?' said Sastrigal.

'Is it proper that you, a teacher, talk like this?'

'That is my reason for dissuading you. Do you know what pension I get? Only ₹78. And I have to get two girls married.'

'What job do you think your Tamil degree will fetch you?' asked Appa.

'We have won our freedom. Now all work will be done in Tamil,' Kesavan said in a feeble voice. It sounded as if he did not have much faith in what he was saying.

'Nonsense! Nothing will change. We will never be able to change our attitude of respecting the English-educated,' said Appa.

'That's the truth! Like ever before, the Sanskrit teacher and the Tamil teacher will be at loggerheads with each other. That will not change as well,' said Sastrigal.

'Just because there's a lot of ill-will between you and Kovizhiyar, why do you assume that to be the rule, rather than an exception?' asked Kesavan, laughing.

'Why does that Kovizhi come and heckle about your studying Tamil? Your father is such a scholar in Sanskrit and you...'

Kesavan did not let Sastrigal to finish the sentence, 'What is it that Sanskrit and Tamil have against each other?'

'It was the white man who created the rift,' said Appa.

'Listen to me, son. Change your course to English MA,' said Sastrigal.

'Sorry! Sir, I have made up my mind to go in for Tamil MA,' said Kesavan.

'Do just as you please. But a Brahmin and ...'even as Sastrigal began his tirade, Appa burst in, 'There you are wrong, Sastrigale! There is no rule which says that a Brahmin should not study Tamil. Come to think of it, every Vaishnavaite has to, per force, be a scholar in both these languages, Tamil and Sanskrit. Only then will he be qualified to call himself one who has studied both versions of Vedanta. I have no objection to your studying Tamil, Kesava! But be assured that the respect that is given to one who has a degree in English or some other subject will not be accorded to a Tamil scholar. Not to a Sanskrit scholar, either. Look around you, there are any number of scholars in Sanskrit. And yet the English educated Radhakrishnan, speaking in English about Sanskrit, is the most acknowledged. You do your degree in Tamil. I'll not stop you. But don't neglect your English. That's all I can tell you, what else?' said Appa.

It was some comfort that Appa did not actively oppose his studying Tamil.

He went to Chidambaram the next morning.

It was arranged for him to stay with Kathiresan, a relative of Murugesan. Kathiresan was in his third year of the Economics Honours course.

'Welcome! Come in,' greeted Kathiresan.

'I do not know how long I am going to be a burden on you,' said Kesavan

'It is no trouble, at all. You have already secured your admission into the University, I suppose.'

'Yes, that is done.'

'Go, meet the warden, he is there in his room. Tell him that if he doesn't allot you a room, you'll have to see the Vice Chancellor.'

'What sort of a man is the Vice Chancellor?'

'Are you a Brahmin?'

'Why do you ask?'

'The VC belongs to the Justice Party. His brother-in-law is Kumbakonam Narayanasami Pillai. Impress on him that you are from Kumbakonam as well. Warden Subrahmanyam is a grumpy, disgruntled man. Generally he helps Brahmins. But you are a Tamil MA student. That's the hitch. He is an English professor, an Iyer from Palghat.'

Subrahmanyam was just what he was described to be. He spat out the words. 'If I say there is no vacancy, I mean there is none. You may do whatever you want. Why do you have to be a Tamil scholar? Will the world come to end if you do not study Tamil?'

Kesavan realised that it was no use trying to make him see sense. He was told that the VC was in his house. Accepting Kathirvelan's suggestion he went to the VC's house, bag and baggage.

He spoke to the watchman at the gate in a tone of fake anxiety and emergency asking to see the VC urgently. The guard did believe it was an emergency and went in to deliver the message.

The VC invited him in. He went in carrying all his belongings with him.

'What's all this?' asked the VC.

'I am a student come here to do my MA in Tamil. Subrahmanya Iyer says there is no vacancy in the hostel. I am from Kumbakonam.'

'Your name?'

'Kesavan.'

'Your father's name?'

He omitted the caste appendage and gave only his father's first name.

'Why has Subrahmanyam refused you admission in the hostel?'

'I was told that he does not like students who do Tamil degrees.'

'Did he tell you that?'

'No, he didn't. Some others told me that.'

The VC was silent for a while.

'What do you think of Periyar marrying now, at this age?'

Kesavan was in a dilemma. On which side was this man? Periyar's or Anna's?

They said that he belonged to the Justice Party. Then he must favour Periyar. Anna did not like the Justice party people. This was a gamble. He had to take a risk.

'I'll not say that what Periyar did was wrong. It is said that in western countries, people of all ages get married to have some kind of companionship. We tend to look at everything from our narrow point of view.'

The man peered at Kesavan for a few minutes. The world seemed to stand still.

Then he took a piece of paper, wrote on it 'admit', put his signature and gave the slip to Kesavan.

19

For a while, the warden, Subrahmanya Iyer kept looking at the chit Kesavan handed him, then looked him up an down as if sizing him up.

'What did you tell the VC?' asked Iyer.

'I told him that I had been admitted into the MA course, but I did not yet get a room in the hostel.

'Did you carry tales about me?'

'No, I just told him what you said, that there was no room available.'

He looked at the slip in his hand once more and then asked, 'Do you belong to the Dravida Kazhagam?'

'I don't think it should bother you,' said Kesavan.

The warden once again gave him a look as if he was assessing Kesavan. It was evident that he was angry, but trying to keep it under check.

'At the moment you will have to share the room with somebody else in a a double room,' said Subrahmanya Iyer looking at the floor.

'Right, that's fine by me.'

'Go to room no 12 in Ilango Block. You will find a quiet boy there, a Brahmin boy. If you can adjust with him and manage to stay there, you are welcome to do so. He is also in the Tamil MA course like you.'

'Thank you,' said Kesavan.

Much like the warden had said, Krishnan appeared to be a quiet boy. By the time Kesavan had paid the hostel charges and came to the room, the warden must have informed Krishnan of his impending arrival. It seemed as if Krishnan was expecting him.

Krishnan had eyes that looked as if they were in a perpetual state of wonder, surprised at everything they saw. He wore thick glasses. He had a thin body.

After Kesavan had put his bedding and box in their places, he shook hands with Krishnan. Krishnan's hand was soft as cotton.

He laughed noiselessly, saying nothing.

Kesavan spread his bedding on the cot. He opened his box, took out a towel and threw it on the back of the chair.

He took out the books and placed them on the table.

Krishnan who had been sitting there pretending not to notice Kesavan's actions, walked up to the table as soon as Kesavan put his books on it. Krishnan picked them up and looked at them. They were all in English. Kesavan realised that there was not a single Tamil book among them.

'Are you not here to do your MA in Tamil?' asked Krishnan laughing.

'Yes. That's right. The warden told me that you had enrolled into that course as well.'

Krishnan was looking through the books keenly as if he had not heard Kesavan's question. Krishnan popped up a question suddenly, 'is your favourite author Balzac?'

'Yes, Shelley and Balzac.'

Krishnan laughed.

'Why this laugh?'

'Nothing in particular.'

'Have you read Balzac?'

A smile was the answer to this question as well.

Kesavan looked at the books Krishnan had kept on his table. They were a mix of English and Tamil books.

Proust, TS Eliot, Stories by Pudumaipithan, Kaivalya Navaneetham, *John O'London's Weekly*....

'Are you also more fond of reading English books?' asked Kesavan

Krishnan responded only with a laugh.

'You laugh all the time, and for everything! Why?'

'I find everything amusing.'

'I have not read Proust.'

'I didn't think you would have.'

'What makes you say that?'

'No reason at all. Have you had your bath? Which mess are you going to eat at?'

'Where do you eat?'

'If you like hot, spicy food, you should go to the Andhra Mess. If you don't, you may eat at the mess where I eat. The choice is yours!'

'I don't like spicy food. But you have not answered my question as yet.'

'What question?'

'I think you know what the question was.'

Krishnan laughed again.

'It is wrong to try and understand each other so completely on this very first day. There must be some suspense,' said Krishnan.

'Trying to analyse a person is wrong, is that what you want to say?'

'You have communist literature, also Balzac, Shelley and Agatha Christie. I don't read Agatha Christie or Edgar Wallace. Did I feel the need to talk about that to you?'

'Is it wrong to read Edgar Wallace?'

'I did not make any such comment, I did not even ask you why you do not have even a single Tamil book.'

Kesavan found it hard to arrive at some opinion of Krishnan.

'Which town do you come from?' asked Kesavan changing the subject.

'Thiruvananthapuram.'

'And you have come all this way from there to study Tamil!'

'Why? What is wrong with that?'

'It is just that I am a little surprised.'

'It is five years since I finished my BA. I went to work after that. Now I am here to do Tamil. More surprises?'

'To speak the truth, yes! You would be familiar with Malayalam too?' Krishnan laughed.

'You laugh a lot.'

'We have been living in Thiruvananthapuram from the days of my grandfather. So, your question made me laugh. There is nothing wrong in your question. What is wrong is that we have lived there from my grandfather's days.' Kesavan looked at him closely.

'Can I ask you something?'

'What do you want to ask?'

'Do you belong to Dravida Kazhagam? '

'Who told you I was?'

'Warden Subrahmanya Iyer. He warned me. 'There is a Dravida Kazahagam boy coming to share your room, has come here with VC's recommendation. Be careful, he might cut the sacred thread that you have on you while you are asleep.'

'Why wait for you to sleep?' asked Kesavan laughing

'A good question. I didn't understand that either. You will not do it, will you?'

'One, I do not have pair of a scissors. Two, I do not belong to Dravida Kazhagam. Three, having the poonool on or not is your problem, your choice. I don't have any right to interfere with your choices. Four, I can guess why the warden cautioned you about me.'

To Krishnan's question, 'Why?' Kesavan told him about his having had to go to the VC to get a place in the hostel

'Are you a Communist?' Krishnan asked after some time.

'Yes,'

'Have you read the book *1984*?'

'No, who is it by?'

'George Orwell. Then there is another book called, *The God that Failed*. That is by Arthur Koestler and Stephen Spender. They were all, at one point in time, communists. So you must read these books.'

'Are you implying that it is wrong to be a Communist?'

'I am not making any judgement. All I say is that you should read these books.'

'And after I have read them...?'

'Nothing will happen. If you are not interested, you need not read them.'

'Do you have them?'

'Yes, I do.'

'Will you lend me those books? May I have them?'

'Not now, later, maybe. Let us go now to eat...'

They went to have their meal. In the dining room, those who were already there kept staring at him. A new boy!

'How are you Pattare?' A boy came to sit by Krishnan's side. Krishnan merely smiled.

'My name is Subramanian, you are new here?' asked the friend of Kesavan.

His Tamil accent smacked of Nanjil Nadu.

'Yes. I am Kesavan.'

'Oh, yes! I saw your name on the list. You are also in the Tamil class, yes?'

'Yes.'

20

$\mathcal{K}$esavan was deep in thought holding *Senavaraiyam* in his hands. About Krishnan....

Kesavan had not met anybody like Krishnan in his entire life at Kumbakonam.

Krishnan was a very shy man, If ever he came across a new face, he would go into his shell like a crab. At the same time he had this extraordinary skill of observing everyone from the wings as it were, and assess their characteristics in an astonishing manner.

Krishnan was well read. He was forever noting things down in a notebook. Whatever he thought was important in any particular book that he read went into it. He had many such notebooks with his comments written in them.

They contained not just interesting comments on the books; but also his own critical analysis of them.

Those notebooks served as his diaries as well.

Kesavan was certain that the notebook would have comments on him, Kesavan, too.

Krishnan kept his notebooks safely under lock and key. Sometimes, he would take out one from them and read.

Krishnan's acquaintance introduced Kesavan to a new literary world.

James Joyce, Ezra Pound, Proust, Arden, TS Eliot, Thomas Mann, Dostoevsky...this new world of theirs raised in him many questions that had no answers or questions that made answers redundant.

Many friends came to their room to meet with Kesavan. They would discuss politics. Krishnan was never a part of these discussions. He would be reading a book, as if unmindful of all that was happening around him. However, when someone said something silly or absurd, the smile on his face would reveal that he was listening in to their conversations even as he read his book.

A routine question that Krishnan asked Kesavan when the others had left the room would be, 'How can you stand this chaff and nonsense?'

'Why not? Do you expect everyone to be an intellectual like you?

'I am no intellectual. My only question is "Do they all have to be compulsive talkers"?'

'What do you mean?'

'You need some kind of sophistication even to be silent. Silence broken can never be whole.'

'It is this ability to vocalise one's thoughts that differentiates humans from other living beings. Language is the most important tool man has to fight and face nature. Freedom is the recognition of necessity. That being the case...'

'Please! All Marxist jargon!'

'Do you mean to say that we have all to stay mute?'

'No, certainly not. With constant usage, many of the words we mouth have become terse and worn out, to the extent of being made to stand naked. The politicians are responsible for having caused this. I feel that Gandhiji's silence at times was only because he had got tired of all these inane words.'

Kesavan laughed and said, 'This is a new theory – I am not sure Gandhiji himself was aware of it.'

'It is not necessary that he know about it.'

'You have notebooks and notebooks, all filled with your writing. Do you mean to say that they are the products of your aversion for words?'

'I do not like words being used to exhibit cleverness. In a way, I should say, I worship words. That is why I get angry when I see them abused. There is no one who adored words more than James Joyce. But, he never used them to showcase his intellect. 'Mother is beastly dead,' – this sentence expresses hatred of a mother as intensely as no one else ever, not even Schopenhauer, could. Here, the words don't matter, only the emotion of hate. If the words had become more important, then it would no longer be literature.'

Kesavan who had always admired authors who had resorted to intellectual play of words, could not accept Krishnan's point of view immediately. He had read all the works of Aldous Huxley. The intelligent use of language that came right through these books had attracted him.

'Your favourite author is Aldous Huxley, so my words may not appeal to you,' said Krishnan.

Kesavan was taken aback. He asked, 'Are you a mind reader?'

Krishnan merely laughed.

'Don't you like Aldous Huxley?'

'Not as a creative writer. I can't accept him as one. The same goes to another favourite author of yours, Balzac.'

'I think, appreciation of men and matters depends a lot on genetic codes. I tried to read the book, you suggested, Baudelaire, try as hard as I could to make some sense of it, I failed. I am not even sure if this is my strength or my weakness.'

'If you are content, resigning yourself to this view, I cannot fault you. If your genetic code is such that it makes you have certain preferences, how can you be blamed? The genetic codes of many of your friends prompt them to wallow in the mire of politics. They relish it very like the pigs that poet Bharati refers to in his poem. How can I say it is wrong?'

'I am a pig too, I enjoy discussions on politics,' said Kesavan.

Krishnan laughed.

Could Kesavan have met a person like Krishnan in Kumbakonam?

Subrahmanya Iyer, perhaps, in his youth was somewhat like Krishnan; but Kesavan remembered Iyer telling him, 'My reading was very much like yours.'

'You seem to be reading "Senavarayam,"' commented Nallaperumal as he came into the room.

Nallaperumal was from Nagerkoil, a student in the final year of his BA Honours course. Indeed he had been praised even by his teachers that any doubt in grammar could be cleared by Perumal.

'Yes, Listen to this. If the commentaries are anything like this who will ever want to study Tamil?' said Kesavan.

'Read it out,' said Nallaperumal.

'The Tholkappiyam couplet seems to be very clear – "If a thing is not available, indicate it by mentioning that something else is available" – that simple. If you go to a shop and ask for rice and the shopkeeper says that he has nothing except salt, then it will be evident that rice is not there. Isn't it just that? Why go into a huge controversy like Senavarayar does, pointing out the flaws in the original work and all that?

'You have got it all wrong. The commentator just says that to let the customer know that what he wants is not available, he should mention a product of the same kind, that if somebody asks for rice, only another grocery item should be mentioned. Senavarayar's question is, is it not possible that one who sells rice, also sells combs? If he does sell combs, then what is wrong in mentioning the comb specifically – that is his argument. But this argument is not acceptable, why would a rice-shop owner sell combs? Instead of combs, he mentions the stone that sucks away snake poison. Will a rice shop stock such a stone?'

Krishnan who had just come in, said, 'Why not? They say such supermarkets exist in the US. There they vend groceries, clothing, stationery, books, toiletries...all in the same shop. Isn't Senavarayar's line of thinking proof enough that there were supermarkets in our country during his time?'

'Somebody asks for rice and all he has to be told is that it is not there, yes? Why go in for all this long-winded explanation?' Even before Kesavan finished his sentence, Nallaperumal butted in, 'Senavarayar also mentions that option.'

'Does one need to study grammar, to ask questions and find answers?' wondered Kesavan aloud.

'You are wrong, look at their competent application of logic, that is what is important here,' said Krishnan.

21

$\mathcal{J}$ust as Kesavan was preparing to go to the dining hall, Narayan Reddy, an engineering student came into their room.

Krishnan gave him a look over.

'Comrade, Good morning! I have come to meet you,' said Reddy as he forcibly shook Krishnan's hands.

'I am not the comrade, he is,' said Krishnan pointing to Kesavan.

'I am sorry! Comrade Kesavan?'

'It is I,' said Kesavan. Kesavan knew who Narayan Reddy was; the president of the Students' Federation. But Reddy did not know Kesavan.

'Comrade Anatharamakrishnan told me of you. The purpose of my visit is that we may be going on a strike from today. If the Vice Chancellor will not accept our demands, we have no other way but to go on a strike.'

'What are your demands?' asked Krishnan.

'They have put up a high wall around the lady's hostel and that prevents the students from walking freely around. That wall must come down.'

'The wall may be a protection for the girls, no?' asked Krishnan.

'No, the intention is to thwart our movement. Many of those girls are members of our party. This wall has come up only to prevent the boys from meeting them. The wall shows that the VC does not trust either the girls or the boys. This is gross injustice and shame inflicted on the entire student community!' Reddy's emotional diatribe came out gushing, half in Telugu and half in English.

He was panting.

'What do the girls feel about it?' asked Kesavan

'The girls are against it.'

'If the wall that separates our boys and girls are pulled down, that will make the communist revolution happen. Right?' asked Krishnan.

Reddy was not sure if Krishnan was serious or trying to be flippant. Krishnan's placid looks made Reddy rule out any mockery.

'You are trivialising the issue,' said Kesavan to Krishnan.

Krishnan gave Kesavan a smile.

'Are you on the VC's side?' asked Reddy of Krishnan angrily.

'Me?' asked Krishnan and laughed again.

'Why do you laugh?'

'He has a very poor opinion of communists,' said Kesavan.

'Me? I have no opinion whatsoever of Indian communists. But I hold the world Marxist thinkers in very high esteem. Even though I cannot accept all that they say, I have no doubt that they were intellectuals of the highest order,' said Krishnan.

'Why is it that you say you have nothing to say about the Indian Communists?'

'Take this issue of a dividing wall. How can this ever warrant a protest to uphold any ideal? A boy wants to be able to meet a girl without any barrier stopping him. Isn't that all that the issue is here? Why do you have to drag in Marx into your petty problems?'

'This is a symbolic protest. The issue of the wall is the limit that has made our anger explode. We don't get good food in the hostel. There are not enough toilets. The warden, the manager, are all swindlers.

Caste feelings are rampant here. The VC is pro-Dravida Kazhagam. Don't you see all these as political issues?'

Just then, a few more students entered the room. They looked quite flustered. Blood was oozing from the corner of a boy's mouth.

'What happened?' asked Reddy.

'The Dravida Kazhagam students are beating up other students!' said one of them.

'Why?'

'The Vice Chancellor has asked the Dravida Kazhagam students to beat our members to prevent the strike.'

'Take this boy to the clinic. Comrade Kesavan! Can you come with me?' asked Reddy.

Kesavan went with him. They hastened towards the engineering college hostel.

A huge ruckus was on.

In addition to the students who belonged to the Dravida Kazhagam party, there were others who had joined in the fray. They were all armed with sticks and whatever weapons they could lay their hands upon...chairs without legs, iron rods, huge stones and the like.

Most of the students had shut themselves up in their rooms.

The armed ones were shouting abuses.

'You go on strike instigated by a "Pappaara" boy? You don't want a Tamilian to be the VC here, is that it?'

This was followed by slogans such as, 'Down with Brahmins!'

On seeing Reddy and Kesavan coming there, some of those who had been shouting came up to them.

'Who are you, trying to do away with our Tamilian? We know that this is a conspiracy that the Congress Brahmins and Communist Brahmins have hatched together. We'll break your legs, mind it!' shouted one of those red-eyed boys.

'This is something to do with students. I don't even know who some of you are,' said Kesavan.

By then Nanmaran who was in the room next to Kesavan's came there.

Nanmaran was a Dravida Kazhagam supporter. He was a pleasant mannered boy. He said, 'Kesavan, you leave this place. These boys from Andhra want to get rid of our VC.'

One among the crowd, pointed to Kesavan and asked Nanmaran, 'He, a Brahmin?'

'He is a Tamil MA student. He is a good boy, though a Brahmin.'

'A Brahmin is a Brahmin – are there any good Brahmins? If you see a snake and a Brahmin, who should you kill? What has our Aiya said, remember?'

'Aiya said nothing of that sort. They are all stories cooked up by one faction. Kesavan, leave this place. Don't join the strikers,' said Nanmaran.

22

Kesavan felt a hard blow fall on him. He could not see who it was that had hit him. He turned around angrily.

'Kesavan, go away! The mob knows no justice,' said Nanmaran.

'Who are you to talk about what is just and what is unjust? A Brahmin appears on the scene and your tone changes. Why is that?' hissed a hefty man with a moustache that matched his form. Kesavan thought that his presence there might be an embarrassment to Nanmaran.

The place where he had been hit ached. But he felt that it would not be possible to argue and put some sense into this crowd which was bent upon violence.

He turned around. Reddy was not to be seen anywhere. He found that he was alone there. Where was Reddy?

Somebody was making an announcement over the microphone.

'There is no strike. Students are asked to attend their regular classes. If they stay away, they will be forcibly taken to the classes. Those who go into hiding will be expelled from the university.'

Kesavan noticed that the one making this announcement did not look as if he was a student. He must have been a party leader.

When Kesavan came back to his room, Krishnan looked at him with a smile on his face.

'A herd of beasts!' said Kesavan.

'Just say herd, that will explain it all.' said Krishnan

'They are holding us to ransom. Do you support the strike?' asked Kesavan.

'If you are a supporter, don't go to your class. But if you are not, attend your class. The crowd has nothing to with this issue,' said Krishnan.

'How can you say that the crowd is of no consequence. If you stay away from the class they say they will carry you bodily into the class room! What right have they to do any such thing?' Krishnan responded with a laugh to Kesavan's outburst.

'What is this laugh for, now?'

'I was just imagining the scene'

'This is no joke, Krishnan. The people from the Kazhagam are beating up one and all. To cap it all they have the support of the VC also.'

'I shall attend my class.'

'That's your will and pleasure. But, if someone wants to stay away, is it fair to force him to attend the classes?'

'You have not answered my basic question. Is it fair to go on a strike just to have a wall brought down? Do you support this point of view?'

'When Reddy came and spoke about it I was not all that sure, I hesitated to accept it, I agree. But things are changed now – so I will support it.'

'Nothing about the basic problem has changed. If you think it is wrong to go on a strike, should you not stick to your policy? I am a Brahmin, one who wears the poonool. So I go to my classes. Not because I am afraid that the Kazhagam people will beat me up, if I don't, but because I think this strike is not right.'

There was clamour outside the room. Kesavan came out of his room to take a look.

'These Kazhagam boys beat up Nallamuthu Sir very badly...we cannot sit quiet anymore!' Dharmavinayagam was frantic.

Nallamuthu was the history professor. He belonged to the Congress party. He wore only khaddar. He had a genial disposition and was always seen with a smile on his face.

Why should he be beaten up? Kesavan could not understand it.

'What happened, Dharmu?' asked Kesavan. Dharmavinayagam was an Economics MA student from Nagerkoil, also of the Congress party.

'Sir just went and asked them why they were resorting to such hooliganism, that was it. The Kazhagam fellows, beat him black and blue. We should not stay quiet any more, destroy them all without any trace; come let's go!' said Dharmu. In no time all the students from in and around Nagerkoil were there to be with Dharmu. They were all armed with whatever they could lay their hands on.

'You are all Congress. Can you be violent, carrying weapons? If Gandhiji had been alive...' Before Krishnan could complete his sentence Dharmu said, 'Pattare! I don't claim to be any Gandhi follower. If somebody gives me two slaps, I'll return them with four.... You stay here mouthing words of right and wrong. They will be here, soon, to cut your poonool off!'

A few students came by with their books in their hands, ready to go their classes.

'The students are on strike today, go back to your rooms!' Dharmu told them.

'Ilavazhagan said there was no strike?'

'Who is your Ilavazhagan to say anything of that sort? I tell you, we are striking, go back to your rooms!'

'This strike is a protest against our VC. It is a strike organised by Andhras, Malayalis and Brahmins. We will not be part of it,' said one of them.

That was enough. His books flew in all directions. A boy from Dharmu's group gave the boy who had spoken against them, a hard slap on his cheek. Those who had accompanied that student ran away.

Before the second hit could fall on that boy, Kesavan intervened, 'Stop it. Let us also not behave like them.'

'Did you see his audacity? See how he talks?'

'Why should this boy be attacked? Let us find his leader. We should make Ilavazhagan with his boys run off from this campus. Come let us go!' said Dharmu.

They ran a few yards raising slogans. Dharmu came back and said, 'Kesavan, you come with us!'

'Can you tell me what this strike is all about?' asked Krishnan.

'The Kazhagam boys have beaten up Nallamuthu Sir. The strike is to protest against that! The VC has got some outsiders to beat up those strikers. We want the VC to resign, the strike is for that as well. Are you satisfied with all these reasons? Do you want any more?'

'I was initially given a different reason...,' said Krishnan with some hesitation.

'I don't know about that! Now this is the reason we want to go on a strike. Pattare! We shall not fight with grass reeds any more. We will not gain anything by that. We have to take knives in our hands. Stop talking unnecessarily about moral values. We don't ask you to join us, we know that you are not strong enough to fight, even with reeds as your weapons.'

'I shall come with you. Will you give me protection?'

Kesavan was surprised at this sudden reversal of Krishnan.

'*Aio*, we don't want you to come with us. I cannot give you any guarantee about safeguarding you either. Give us your blessings, that should be enough,' said Dharmu.

'Where do we go now?' asked Kesavan.

'To the Arts Faculty. I hear that the Kazhagam fellows are gathered there. Comrades are also with us. And you are a comrade, right? I forgot to mention the purpose of this attack, we are going to pay back in full for the beatings that Nallamuthu Sir got from them.'

'Beating up the students cannot be an action plan. Let us go, meet with the VC. Ask him to suspend the student who beat up Nallamuthu

Sir. If he refuses to do that, then we shall consider our future course of action.

'You are no different from Krishnan.'

'I feel that this is the right kind of protest to make, should we repeat their mistakes?'

'Anna! Kesavan is right. That will tear the mask the VC wears before the world, yes?'

As they came out of the hostel gate, a group led by Reddy joined them. Dharmu told Reddy about Kesavan's suggestion.

'This is just what I had in mind. Kesavan is a communist and so, it is no surprise that the same idea has occurred to him. Moreover, Dharmu, the Kazhagam fellows have gone into hiding. The Arts Faculty is empty. We are coming from there. Let us go to Nallmuthu Sir's house and garland him first. Then, with his blessings, we shall go to meet the VC,' said Reddy.

'No, let us not drag Nallamuthu Sir into all this. I don't think it is proper to create an embarrassing situation for him,' said Kesavan.

'But did they not beat him up?' asked Reddy.

'I know for sure that Nallamuthu Sir will not like our going to his house. Please, let us meet the VC on his behalf and apprise him of how Sir got beaten. The VC cannot ignore the fact that the Kazhagam men have attacked Sir. This is our opportunity. If he refuses to take action against the miscreants then we will demand his resignation,' said Kesavan.

They proceeded towards the VC's house, shouting slogans along the way.

It was decided that Dharmu, Reddy, Kesavan and two other students meet with the VC and talk to him. But when they went there, a surprise awaited them.

Policemen were jumping off some four or five vans, clicking their boots noisily.

23

$\mathcal{A}$ stern-looking sub-inspector walked towards them. It appeared as if with just one look he could scorch the students.

He did not come alone. Two policemen flanked him. The policemen wielded guns. The sub-inspector spoke in a gruff voice, 'You cannot gather here. There is a ban on it. So go away without creating any trouble.'

Kesavan said, 'We are not here to make trouble. We just want to meet the Vice Chancellor. Once we have seen him, we shall go away.'

'You cannot see the VC now.'

'Let the VC tell us that he will not see us. Who gave the right to policemen to tell us that we cannot meet the VC?' asked Dahrmavinayagam.

'The VC has told me not to let any student in,' said the Sub-Inspector.

'We will not go without seeing him. Just five of us will go in.' said Kesavan. The sub-inspector thought for a few minutes.

Some Dravida Kazhagam student leaders and some outsiders – VIPs from the party – were standing in the portico.

'It is not fair! The Kazhagam students have been allowed to go in and they will not let us in. We will see this matter to its end,' said Dharmavinayagam angrily.

'Let us all go in, ignoring the police injunction. Let them know what a student revolution is!' said Reddy in English.

'That would be foolish. Let us see what the Inspector comes out with. He has gone inside the VC's room,' said Kesavan to Reddy. Dharmu looked at the students who had accompanied them and said, 'Don't stand silently! Keep up your slogans!'

A whole-hearted cry of, 'Down with the Vice Chancellor!' was raised.

The sub-inspector walked hurriedly up to them. 'The VC will see only three of you. Decide who among you should go in,' he said.

It was decided Reddy, Dharmavinayagam and Kesavan would go in.

When the three entered the VC's room they were surprised to see him sitting bare-chested, clad only in a lungi. Against the dark background of his neck, a gold chain glittered.

He was not alone. Two huge Alsatian dogs stood on either side of him like the lion statues beside a throne.

The VC was stroking the dogs lovingly.

'Yes! Tell me, what brings you all here?' asked the VC.

'It will be easier for us to talk to you if you could send these dogs away,' said Kesavan.

'The dogs will not go anywhere. They will stay here with me, you can tell me what you have come to speak to me about,' roared the VC.

Silence prevailed there for a few moments.

'Why are you silent? Speak, if you have something to say,' said the VC.

'We were not sure if it was the dogs barking or you talking. That's why we hesitated to speak,' said Dharmu.

'You dare laugh at me? Get out!' when the VC shouted, his dogs growled with him, as if in accompaniment.

'You have the police outside, the dogs inside. Are you trying to intimidate us?'

'Why should I be afraid of you? You make trouble when the

management builds a wall round the ladies' hostel to give them better security, you protest that the wall should not be built. And you go on a strike just for this. What are you all here for, to get your education or to gallivant with the girls?' asked the VC.

'Don't make the issue appear vulgar. You have put up the wall as if you have no trust in us, boys. We see it as a blur on our character. The next demand is that we do not have enough toilets and bathrooms. When that is more of an urgent need, why spend on a wall?' spoke Reddy.

The VC interrupted Kesavan who began, 'And there is one more thing....'

'The wall has come up only because the girls came to me with their complaints. If the boys had behaved decently, this problem would not have cropped up at all,' said the VC.

'Not a single girl from that hostel wants this wall. They have all signed a declaration to that effect. Here it is,' Reddy said as he took out a sheet of paper from his pocket and handed it to the VC. The big man tore the paper up without as much as a glance at it.

Kesavan said, 'There is another important matter that I have been trying to tell you. The Dravida Kazhagam students have beaten up the true Gandhian Professor Nallamuthu. And having done this atrocity, I see them here, in the portico of your house, come to advise you of the happening. What action are you going to take against those students?'

The VC was silent for a while. Then he peered into the neck of his dog on one side of him, carefully picked a tick and stroked the animal gently. The dog responded with a grateful wag of its tail.

Kesavan had a doubt: Was this man going to set the dog on them?

'I come from an old Congressman's family. My grandfather can go straight to the CM and talk to him. He can tell the CM that you are partial to the Kazhagam students,' said Dharmu.

'Who might your grandfather be?' asked the VC. Kesavan thought that his voice revealed a shade of anxiety.

'I don't think I need to tell you his name,' said Dharmu.

'You cannot scare me with all these names. Nallamuthu was a fool to go, abuse the students and get beaten up. I cannot be held responsible for all this. Don't you dare blackmail me like this. I take actions only after I have consulted the CM. You have all to vacate the hostel immediately, get out of this place within 24 hours. I am closing the university. If you create any trouble, the police are there to deal with you. Just get out now,' said the VC and got up.

When the three came out of the room, the policemen stood at attention with their guns held straight, as if they were ready to meet any emergency.

'What do we do now?' asked Reddy.

'Nothing, I suppose! The students who came with us are all gone. Just the three of us here, now,' said Kesavan.

They first went to Reddy's hostel. They found the students packing up, vacating their rooms and getting ready to leave the premises. Reddy shouted angrily. 'So our protests stop here!'

None of them gave him a reply. Dharmu and Kesavan went to Professor Nallamuthu's house.

Nallamauthu was reclining on his easy-chair. There were bandages on his forehead and left arm.

The professor welcomed the two boys with a wry smile.

His wife was giving his back a hot fomentation.

'Are these students or evil *Rakshasas*?' asked the professor's wife.

'We went to see the VC and told him how the Kazhagam fellows beat you up,' said Kesavan.

'What did he say?' asked Nallamuthu in a feeble voice.'

'He says that you abused the students. You are from a family of Congressmen, if only you went to the CM and ...,' even before Dharmu had finished his sentence, Nallamuthu said, 'After independence, the true Congressman has lost all respect. Something like this, a grave misdeed, happened in our village. My brother went to Madras Fort to apprise the CM of the incident. But those who are now in the Fort, are only interested in votes, not in justice or injustice! Gandhiji knew what would happen after independence and that was the reason he suggested the Congress party be disbanded. If some of us who are upright, wish to preserve our dignity. We have to move away from mainstream politics, we have no other choice.'

'The VC says that he took action only after he had consulted the CM, do you think it is true?' asked Dharmu.

'Quite possible, he did,' said Nallamuthu.

'What do you think we should do now?' asked Kesavan.

'Better go home, most of the students have already left. What can you do against this large posse of policemen?' said Nallamuthu.

Kesavan came back to his room, a picture of dejection.

Krishnan welcomed him with a smile, 'Tell me, soldier! We go home now, right?'

Without giving him any reply, Kesavan looked out. A policeman was snuffling out a cigarette he had finished smoking, with his boot.

In a burst of sudden anger and helplessness, Kesavan banged his fist hard on the table.

24

When Kesavan got back home, his father was in the hall.

The look he gave his son, seemed to say that he was expecting Kesavan to come home. This surprised Kesavan a little.

After looking at him, his father bent down and got engrossed in the book he had been reading.

Kesavan felt that his father wanted to ask him something. His look seemed to give Kesavan that impression.

As he was about to go upstairs, his mother came in from the backyard.

Kesavan expected she would ask, 'Hey! Why this sudden visit?' but she did not ask him anything.

After giving her son a nervous look, she turned her eyes on his father.

Kesavan went upstairs.

Would Appa have heard about the things that happened at the university? Kesavan put his box in his room and went to stand in the veranda.

He wondered how he could deal with Appa if the old man was already in the know of things.

An active card game was going on at the front thinnai of the Tahsildar's house.

'Here is the trump card,' said Kudai Sarangan, throwing the card on the floor with a flourish and giving the others a look of triumph.

Kesavan felt his mother standing behind him.

'They are short of a hand. Perhaps you are here to fill the vacancy,' said Amma.

He sensed the mockery in her voice. That meant she was aware of, at least, some of what had happened. Her source of information could only have been Appa. Appa's pregnant silence made sense now. He turned to look at her.

'Rajam, a regular one of that card-playing gang, has been transferred to Bombay and has left this town. So they were talking yesterday, that they were short of one player,' said Amma.

'I don't know to play cards.'

'Go, sit with them; they will teach you.'

'Why do I have to play cards?'

'You are expelled from the university. What are you going to do now?'

Kesavan stared at his mother.

'What do you mean? Expelled from the university? Who has been sent out?'

'You! Appa got a letter from the university yesterday.'

He did not come to Kumbakonam after the university was declared closed. He had gone to Chennai with Reddy for a couple of days. So, the university had been rather active in the meantime, he thought.

'What did Appa say?'

'What can he say? He'll just say, "enough of this studying, stay at home" – what else?'

'What am I supposed to do, sitting at home?'

'See them there? Join them for card games. Come home for meals, what else? The university has sent you home, what else can you do?'

'I'll talk to Appa and...' before Kesavan could continue, Amma interrupted him and said, 'Look here! Appa is very angry. Don't pick up a quarrel with him now. Just accept that what you did was wrong.'

Kesavan came down without giving Amma any reply.

He stood in front of his father.

'Was there any letter from my university?' asked Kesavan. Appa removed his gaze from the book and looked at him for a moment; then he went back to his book.

'Amma says that there's some letter.'

'Yes! What do you plan to do now?' asked his father in a very calm tone. This surprised Kesavan no end.

He did not expect this question. More than the question, the patient tone surprised him. He had come expecting fireworks; he was a little disappointed.

'What I am to do? Go back and study, of course!'

'It doesn't look like you went there to study! Looks like you went there to create trouble otherwise why would the university suspend you?'

'The VC is a Dravida Kazhagam man – he...'

'He sent you out because you are the model of a Brahmin. Is that what you are trying to say? Trying out some cock and bull stories on me, are you?'

'Appa, listen! The students at the university do not have proper facilities. The fee is high. When we went to him with all these problems he threatened us with police action. Not just this, there is this very good professor, the Dravida Kazhagam fellows went and beat him up. The VC has not taken any action on those students.'

'Look, here is a report in today's paper about your strike. Your VC's report is something, very different from what you say. Read it,' saying this, he picked up the newspaper – *The Hindu* – that was on the floor by the side of his easy chair and gave it to Kesavan. He had already read it that morning.

'This is all cooked up. It is true that we said it was wrong to raise a wall. Doesn't this mean that they do not have any faith in the students? Will a wall ensure that everyone behaves properly?'

'I don't care about all that. Enough of your studying, that's all,' said Appa in a firm voice as he got up from the easy chair.

'Not study?' Kesavan also had raised his voice a little.

'You have a BA degree? Whatever job you get that is enough.'

'What job will a Brahmin with a BA degree get?'

'What will a Brahmin with a MA Tamil get? Your joining in that Tamil MA course is just a waste. You will be the only Brahmin in this entire presidency to go in for a Tamil MA course. Who will give you any job?'

'We are not going to spare the VC. We have sent a representation to the Chief Minister. Many members of the Assembly will soon come up with questions about the propriety of a Dravida Kazhaga man being allowed to do what he wants, when the Congress is at the helm of affairs!'

'Let them ask their questions. You need not go there to study anymore, that's it!'

'Appa! How can you speak like this? What is the meaning of your decision?'

'I'll be saving some money, that's what it means.'

'You have often said that if a man does not have just anger, he is not fit to be called a man. Now, why don't you try and understand the justice in my anger?'

'What is just in your anger? You say you should not be stopped from going to the place where ladies are, is that just anger?'

'Nobody ever wanted that. You should see the wall, only then will you know the kind of opinion that VC has of women. He is even known to have said that, each and every girl comes to study here only to look for a husband. What a low, despicable line of thinking!'

'What is the VC's subject?'

'Biology.'

'Maybe that's why he looks at the issue from a biological angle. Who can ignore the biological instincts?' said Appa.

Kesavan did not expect his father to speak in that manner.

Appa went inside and came back with the letter he had received from the university.

It was his suspension order; it said that unless he apologised for his action, he would not be readmitted into his college. The letter was addressed to him and a copy of it had been sent to his father.

'Do you know who your VC is ?'

'His name?'

'No, not his name, I am talking about the kind of person he is. He is the brother-in-law of the Justice Party leader from Banathurai, Narayanasami Pillai.'

'Is that so?'

'Sabesan was here yesterday. He said that this man is a thorough scoundrel. He will be up to anything. Why don't you go to Madras and do your MA in English?'

'What is wrong with my studying Tamil?'

'Brahmins are hounded. Tamil is the DMK domain. What are the chances of your getting into any job? I think Sabesan is right.'

'Do you mean to say that Brahmins do not have any connection with Tamil? There is one Krishnan in my class...a Brahmin, he is....'

'I am not talking about that. Are you going to finish your studies and be without any job?. I have no objection to your doing that. The lessees are all out to swindle me. If you will take up farming, employing a few farm hands, that's all right by me. We can all go back to Kodaivasal.'

Kesavan was shocked. Does Appa really entertain such ideas?

'My objections are not what you would suppose them to be; I want to prove that a Brahmin can study Tamil and come up in life. It is easy for me to accept defeat and go to Madras, do an English degree. But I cannot accept my suspension order lying down. What wrong did I do, that I got suspended?'

'What do you intend to do? You are tendering your apology?'

'No! We have represented against the VC's actions. Let us see what happens!'

'Nothing will happen! When all men are just and either due to their carelessness or their oversight a wrong gets done and when another man fights it with a feeling of just anger, then there are chances of things being set right. But when a man deliberately does something wrong, then what can just anger do against it? Sheer waste, it would be!' said Appa.

His words set Kesavan thinking.

25

*N*ext morning when Kesavan came down from his room upstairs, Appa was reciting the *Thiruppavai* verses in the *Puja* room.

To coincide with the Christmas vacation in December, the university got closed some four days earlier.

If any action was to be taken it was possible to do it only after the holidays. Would it be possible to do anything at all? This question had tormented his mind the whole of the previous night. He couldn't sleep properly.

He went to the wellhead, washed his face and came back into the kitchen. Amma's mouth was also uttering the Thiruppavai verses in a softer tone.

'Go, have your bath, I'll give you your coffee.'

He went to the front side to see if the newspaper had been delivered.

Someone was sitting on the thinnai. He looked older than Appa and had Appa's looks. He was surprised; who was he?

'Who do you want?'

No reply.

He seemed to be lost in space. His face was expressionless; he sat there, not moving, like a statue.

'Who are you? Who do you want?' asked Kesavan once again.

No reply.

Was he dumb or deaf? Kesavan did not know what to do.

He went closer to the man and asked again, 'Who do you want?'

He did not look at Kesavan at all! Perhaps he found the vacant space more interesting!

The caste mark on his forehead was half wiped out. He had on a dirty *veshti* and a towel.

Once upon a time he must have looked handsome. But now his body was withered and a sort of melancholy could be seen in his eyes.

Kesavan picked up the paper and went inside.

Amma who came into the hall then said, 'Now, don't you sit here with the paper. Go, have your bath.'

'Some stranger is sitting on the thinnai. I asked him who he was, but he does not say anything.'

'He is your *periappa*.'

'My periappa?'

'Yes!'

'Where was he all these years?'

'You go have your bath first, then we can talk about other things.'

Kesavan was surprised. Why had anyone not mentioned this man ever before? Why had he turned up there all of a sudden?

'Amma, is he deaf or dumb? You ask him questions and he sits there as if he has not heard you!'

'He is neither deaf nor dumb. He has had his spin and is all spent now. You go for your bath now.'

What does she mean, 'all spent'? One more black sheep in the family? How many of them did the family have? It was obvious that Amma was not very happy at this man landing at their house.

It looked as if Appa had accepted the newcomer. He was gradually realising that his assessment of his father had not been all that correct.

He had his bath, had his coffee and came out of the kitchen. Appa was sitting in the hall reading his newspaper.

Appa gave him a look-over.

'Who is that sitting on our thinnai outside? Amma says he is my periappa,' said Kesavan

'Yes.'

'How is it that I did not even know that I had a periappa?'

Appa did not reply.

Soundaram came in then. Kesavan knew that Soundaram was some relative of his from his father's side. But he was not sure what exactly the relationship was. Kesavan remembered that Soundaram called his father Chithiya. Then, perhaps, the man sitting outside was Soundaram's father. But on all those many visits to Soundaram's house he had never ever seen this man there.

'So, Chithiya, you seem to be entertaining your Muththa, elder brother? Shouldn't you beat him and drive him off?' Soundaram asked angrily as he came into the hall.

'Keep your mouth shut! Don't make me angry. I am warning you!' said Appa, his voice not losing any of its calm.

'This man has had his fun and now has turned up at your doorstep like a bad penny, a pauper and a beggar!. Do you consider it fair?'

'He did not come here of his own accord. I brought him here. He was sitting outside the Ramaswami temple. I didn't want the honour of our family to come down to the street and into the open so I brought him home.'

'How rich he was! And he squandered it all! Now I am rotting here as a Vakil's clerk.'

'You don't have to do anything for him. I shall take care of him. Neither need your brothers worry about taking care of him. I take on the responsibility,' said Appa.

'You talk of my brothers. Are they in any better financial condition than I am? Anna is in a brass vessel shop, tinkering with the vessels there. Thambi is in a cloth shop tearing off lengths of materials. And who is responsible for all that? Your dear Muththa? Yes? If he had given us some sort of education, would we be in such a sorry state? He spent all his time in his prostitute's house, that was his ultimate heaven – *Vaikuntam*. How, then could his family become anything? Now, when he has not a paisa on him, they have all driven him into the streets. He has come to take refuge in the temple. Chithia, don't mistake me, I really wonder, what do you owe him? Nothing at all!'

Appa was silent.

Amma came in bringing the *prasadam*. 'Here, Soundaram, have some prasadam.

'Chithi, looks like your brother-in-law is visiting you!' said Soundaram as he took the prasadam from Amma's hand.

Amma did not reply.

Soundaram sat on the bench.

'Why doesn't he speak anything?' asked Kesavan of Soundaram.

'What can he speak about? You ask him how to spend a wealth of forty *velis* of land. Perhaps, he will then tell you how to do it.'

'That much land?'

'Oh, yes! Did you not know about it? He is the son of your grandfather's first wife. Your father is the son of the old man's second wife. This man was given away in adoption. He inherited forty velis of land. Not even a trace of anything is left now. Here I am a clerk in a Vakil's office mouthing a thousand lies everyday, to just earn my meal.'

All that he heard shocked Kesavan. He was not aware of any of these connections. Three wives! And two sons given away in adoption! Chithappa who died some time ago and now this periappa! How similar their lives seem to have been!

Kesavan knew that Appa had lost his father when he was a mere five-year-old. He had also heard of all the alliances the old man had had right from Nachiarkoil up to Kodavasal. Appa was just the opposite of his father. Some of his relations would also talk about how Appa had carefully preserved whatever had been spared of the family wealth, wealth that had escaped the pleasure-loving Thatha's clutches, prevented the family from coming to the streets and upheld the family's prestige as well. Perhaps Appa's brothers had continued in Thatha's footsteps, taking care to preserve the notorious name of being rakes. To squander forty velis of land! That was something, indeed!

Appa, however, had not vented his anger at his brother and had chosen to bring him home! That was a marvel! Appa was different, no doubt, Kesavan decided.

'What if there is talk that the sons did not feed him?' Soundaram was asking Appa

'What does it matter if the son takes care of a man or the brother?' said Appa.

'My mother, didn't she spend a whole lifetime in tears! Who was responsible for that? Now, today you want to entertain him, you think it is fair?'

'All three of you, brothers, tossed your mother from one to another, what kind of justice was that? Don't you dare talk of great issues like justice and injustice! He is now here. If and when he makes his exit from this world, I'll send word to you. You can come and do the last rites. Just go now!' Appa was telling Soundaram, when Periappa walked in.

He looked alternately at Appa and Soundaram.

'Are you hungry? Will you eat?' asked Appa.

He did not say anything.

He sat on the floor.

He kept staring at Appa fro some time. Then suddenly he broke into sobs.

Appa went up to him, sat beside him and said, 'What is this? Don't be silly! Stop crying. Is there anyone who has not committed any mistake? Maybe, you have erred what is the use of crying over it now? Stop crying, calm yourself. We are all here for you,' said Appa.

'Excellent play acting!' said Soundaram.

'Will you keep your mouth shut?' Appa shouted angrily.

Soundaram got frightened.

Periappa stopped crying and looked at Appa with gratitude.

Kesavan went upstairs.

Appa's form appeared large on his mental screen, like he was seeing a *Visva Roopam*. His eyes filled with tears of pride for his father.

He wished he could be a worthy son of such a noble father.

Henceforth, achieving that would be his life's goal.

Soundaram entered his room.

'Why don't you try to convince your father, about what he should do?' asked Soundaram.

'Convince him of what?'

'It is a mistake to even let that man come inside the house. They say that in Andavan's Periyashramam, they give shelter to destitute Vaishnavaite Brahmins, give them food, a place to stay and all that. We shall also give whatever we can towards the expenses, if your father wants to contribute, let him. Let your Periappa go and live there. I don't think it is proper that your father should want to have him live here with him.'

'What can be your objection to my father wanting to let him stay here?'

'He is a bad man, a wastrel who spent all our wealth on evil ways. No mercy should ever be shown to him.'

'It is not nice to hear you talk like this about your own father.'

'If you were also abandoned like us and ended up as we are now, you wouldn't talk any different. He had a good English education. But did he give us a good education? Even your father got educated on his own.'

'Periappa had an English education?'

'Oh, yes! He did. He has a BA degree from this very Kumbakonam College. He must be the only educated one to get into all those bad ways. All those who went to college with him are millionaires today, famous lawyers and the like. Here is this man, begging for his food at your door.'

Kesavan was shocked. Periappa did not look like he had a BA degree; and that too a degree in those days when it was not all that common. His adopted father must have sent him to college because, perhaps he had wanted this adopted son to become a famous lawyer.

'It is a great surprise that he is, indeed, educated.'

'They say he came first in the Presidency in his BA. Then he went to Madras to study law. There he got into all sorts of bad habits...drinks, prostitutes, the whole works. All the while we were here, orphans. This man did not care to even come and find out how we were. Rogue!'

'How come? Were you all born even before he went to Madras to study law?'

'We were all born even while he was doing his BA. He went to Madras and got lost there! He never came back!'

'And why did he do that?'

'Only he knows why he did what he did.'

'Do you know for sure that he squandered the money on drinks and women?'

'That's what they say. The rumour also goes that he was going round with a white lady and left all his property to her, having trusted her so wholeheartedly. Nobody knows what really happened. All we know is that we are paupers.'

Kesavan thought that probably Periappa was a different kind of person altogether.

26

Kesavan tried his best to get Periappa to open up. But the man would not budge. How could this man be silent the whole day? Come to think of it, this was also a kind of Yoga, meditation.

He sat on the thinnai and appeared to stare at the street. There would be no expression on his face whatsoever. It was not even that he was watching all that was happening on the street. Nothing that happened around him seemed to penetrate to him.

'The backyard is free, go bathe,' Appa would say and then he would go and have his bath.

Appa had to call Periappa for his meals. Kesavan tried a couple of times to call him to come in and eat. But when he continued to sit there silently, Kesavan got irritated.

Kesavan gave *The Hindu* for Periappa to read. But the man took the paper and put it beside him. He did not read the paper.

'Will you not read the paper?'

Silence!

'Do you think that there is nothing worthwhile in there?'

Silence!

'I have seen you talk to my father. Why won't you talk to me?'

Silence!

'I want to know about you.'

It was like knocking against a rock. The man never opened his mouth.

A couple of days later, when Kesavan was walking through Big Street, he met with Kudai Sarangan there. Sarangan's cheek was bulging with the betel leaf mixture. When he spoke with his head raised a little to prevent the juice from his mouth from spilling out, Kesavan, cautiously, maintained a safe distance from the man, afraid that the spittle from Sarangan's mouth might get sprayed on him.

'Your Periappa, installed now on your thinnai, is he dumb?'

'I don't know.'

'How is it that you don't know? Have you never heard him speak?'

'I don't know if he speaks to Appa or not. He has never said a word to me.'

'He looks like some *Mahan*, an enlightened person.'

'Is that so?'

'Only those who savour life to the full become yogis, giving up everything. Arunagirinathar, for example. Have you seen the movie *Chintamani*? Bhagavathar acts in the role of a character like your Periappa, the role of one who after years of running after women becomes a great yogi. You would not have seen that movie, *Chintamani*. *Haridas* was another movie with the same Bhagavathar acting.'

'How do you claim that Periappa is a Mahan?

'Such great people don't talk. Silence has that kind of power. I went and stood by your Periappa and said, '*Namaskaram mama!*' The radiance on his face just dazzled me. Blinded by it I shut my eyes. I told Thalayatti about it. He said he also had a similar experience. But when I told your Appa about it, he shooed us off, saying, 'Don't you waste your time.'

'What are you trying to imply?' asked Kesavan, a little anxious.

'The sage in your house belongs to humanity at large. Your father should not keep him locked up like this. He should be allowed to give *Darshan* to one and all in the Agraharam,' said Sarangan, spitting out some betel juice.

He then wiped his mouth with the towel he had on his shoulder. Kesavan was shocked.

He realised that a new tale was being spun.

'Mama, he is no sage or saint. After throwing away huge amounts of money, he now sits in our house, a mere pauper. Don't make of him an Arunagirinathar or Tulsidas; he is not one to sing *Thiruppugazh* or *Ramayana*,' said Kesavan.

'He does not need to compose *Ramayana* or *Thiruppugazh*. All we need is just a benevolent look from him. Yesterday, or maybe the day before, Aravamudhu came to meet your father. He saw your Periappa outside your house and asked him, 'How are you mama?' your Periappa merely lifted his arm. Just that. Aravamudu who has been complaining of a nagging pain in the pit of his stomach, who has consulted any number of doctor without getting any relief, was rid of his pain the instant your Periappa raised his hand! What do you say to this? He is a sage, there's no doubt about it.'

Kesavan felt a rage overtake his head.

'Look here, Mama! Don't you come up with some concoction like this and get crowds to mob our house,' said Kesavan in a firm tone.

'You are a Communist, you do not have faith in these matters. Your father seems to be becoming an atheist as well. We are people who believe. In Kali yuga, we believe that God does not incarnate as he did in the previous ages. He comes as an ordinary man and relieves us all of our problems. I don't know if your Periappa is God or not. But he is a godsend, a gift to our Sannidhi Street.'

Kesavan realised that there was no point in continuing the conversation. He went home and told Appa about his meeting Sarangan.

Appa heard him out silently. Soundaram who was present there, also listened to Kesavan's account with his face aglow with happiness.

'You should put a stop to this madness immediately. You must call

the people of this street and tell them all about Periappa, otherwise...'
Before Kesavan could finish his sentence, Soundaram butted in, 'What
should the people be told?'

'Tell them that he is just an ordinary man, not any saint. His
wife died, after an entire life spent in shedding tears. He did not do
anything to get his children educated!' Soundaram raised his hand to
stop Kesavan's speech.

'I told you the same thing the other day. Then you supported your
father, now you speak ill of your periappa,' said Soundaram.

'I am not saying anything against him. The people of this street
want to use him for their own selfish reasons.'

'And what would that selfish reason be?' asked Soundaram.

'To disgrace me,' said Appa.

'Why would they want that?' asked Soundaram.

'Because I know the true worth of each one on this street. One
swindles the temple money, another pretends to be very orthodox but
has abetted a Mohammaden from Thukkampalayam street to forge a
relationship with that man's own sister-in-law. Now they are trying
to put me, one who is really a god-fearing man, in some sort of fix.'

'How would you be put to any trouble, Chithiya?' asked Soundaram.

'I'll, certainly, be in some delicate situation. Is your father any
saint? I took pity seeing him hungry, sitting in front of the temple and
brought him home. Now these wastrels want to make him a saint and
make some money on the side. I'll not allow that to happen.'

'We'll get the money,' said Soundaram with a smile.

'What did you say?' Appa's angry voice came loud and menacing.
Appa's tone scared Soundaram. He was quiet for sometime.

'You want to con the people of this town, isn't that what you are
saying?' asked Appa.

'I don't mean to deceive anybody. But if people will get conned,
how am I to be blamed?'

'What kind of logic is this?'

'This is neither logic nor any unreasonable argument. All these days we did not get anything from our father. Now, when this chance for us to make some money appears, why do you want to put spokes in the wheels?'

'The other day you abused me for harbouring him. Now you have found a use for your father and want him, is that it?'

'I don't want him. I don't say I am going to take him away from here...let him be here. When the crowd begins to gather and some puja and other such things get performed, if any money comes voluntarily in, hand it over to me. That's all we want. I know you will not touch any of that money. But we need money, what is to be done? What is wrong in my suggestion, you tell me Chithiya,' said Soundaram laughing.

Only then, did Kesavan notice that Amma had been standing there all the time. Amma did not have any opinion of her own. It was her unshakeable conviction that whatever Appa said would be right.

'What is there for me to say? One thing I am sure of. After having played around to his heart's content, now this thinnai seems to be his only refuge. I cannot accept that this poor Brahmin be projected as some great saint and all that!' Having said her say she looked at Appa to solicit his approval. A smile broke on Appa's face. That meant he approved.

'He is no saint, a fact we are all aware of. But only a fool will let some advantage that he may get slip out of his hands, said Soundaram.

'Will you leave this place now, before my anger crosses its limits?' said Appa.

'OK, Then! I'll take my father with me,' said Soundaram in a decisive voice.

'I won't let you do that. Don't torture him, you rogues!' said Appa.

27

*W*hen Kesavan woke up the next morning, the sun was way up in the sky, making the room bright with its light. He got up with a sudden spurt of energy to look at the clock. It showed seven-thirty.

He was surprised that Amma had not come to wake him up. Then he remembered that Appa would have gone early in the morning to Kodavasal to attend a wedding. Appa had asked Kesavan to go with him, but Kesavan had refused. Periappa was there in the house and so Amma could not go with Appa.

Appa had asked him the previous evening,' When do you think your university will reopen? What about you? Are you going back there or are you planning to discontinue your studies?'

Kesavan had not said anything.

Appa had continued, 'I am not sure what you can achieve by doing your Tamil MA. Just go to Kodavasal and supervise the land cultivation there. The lessees are always out to cheat me. Or if you want to study something else, do that. I have no objection to that either. But wherever you are, don't get into strikes and all that anymore.'

'I have been suspended, so I have to see this issue to its end.

Only then will I be able to decide what I can do,' Kesavan had replied.

'All seems to be quiet on that front. There is no news about your university in the newspapers either. They are keeping the university closed and nobody seems to be doing anything about it. You go and get your certificates. That is all you should do now,' said Appa.

'I hear that the university is to reopen on the eighth of next month. I certainly shall go there then and continue my studies there,' Kesavan had declared.

He had reassured Appa with his decision. But, will that happen? Will the University take back the suspended students? What if it insists on apology letters? What will the other student leaders do? If they all agree to apologise, will he be able to, stand alone and not succumb to the coersion? If he did not comply, what would happen to his studies?

All these thoughts went round and round in his mind, keeping him awake until very late the previous night. As he rolled up his bed and was about to go downstairs, Amma came up panting.

'Kesava! Look at this! There's a huge crowd gathered in front of our house!' said Amma.

'Why are they here?' asked Kesavan.

'Appa has gone out of town. I don't know what we are to do. Come down quickly and see what it is all about.'

Kesavan hurried down. A crowd stood outside their door. Since Amma had locked the wooden gate, they could not come in.

Periappa was on the thinnai staring into space as usual. Kesavan went out.

'What do you all want?'

'They are all here to have a darshan of your Periappa. Open the gate,' said Kudai Sarangan.

'Mama! This is not right. Periappa sits there quietly. Why do you all want to trouble him,' asked Kesavan

'Are you talking sense? You have a saint in your house and you prevent us all from having his darshan, that is a great sin! We will leave this place only after we have had his darshan,' said Thalayatti. There would have been around fifty people out there. On all their faces was a mixture of fear, excitement and expectation.

'Do you know that Appa has gone out of town?' asked Kesavan.

'No, we didn't know that. Where has he gone?' asked Kudai Sarangan.

'Why do you pretend as if you didn't know that Appa was not here. You are all here, only because you are aware of his not being at home. When Appa is not around, without his permission, I shall not agree to anything. Appa is very angry at you making a saint of Periappa. So, just go away, each to your business' said Kesavan angrily.

'Who is this small boy to order us!' Kondu of the last house said and came to the gate and gave it a hard shake.

Kondu's full name was Kothandam. It was a mystery how without any education and without any inherited wealth, Kondu went round in the town as if he was the son of a rich landlord. Kesavan had, however, unravelled this mystery a year before. The man was a police informer. They said that this work brought him a good income. There had been a municipal election a few months earlier. A popular pickle industry magnate had contested the elections. He was a Brahmin. Kondu opposed him then.

Afraid that the Brahmin votes would get distributed, the Brahmin elites tried to persuade Kondu to withdraw his application. But Kondu was unyielding.

Just a couple of weeks before the election Kondu disappeared. The pickle magnate won the election. Many wondered how Kondu suddenly managed to acquire a motorcycle.

Seeing Kondu shaking the gate so forcefully, Kesavan came out and stood before Kondu.

'What you are doing, is not right. It is good that you have all suddenly developed this desire to have the darshan of a great man. But Appa is not in town and I can not let any of you come in now,' said Kesavan

'Some green horn that you are, stopping us! I can enter this house with the policemen in attendance. You just open the door and let whoever wants to have the darshan have it,' said Kondu stroking the gold chain around his neck.

'No! I cannot let you in!' said Kesavan and went inside the house.

A loud noise was heard. The gate was broken and it came crashing down – many from the crowd rushed in with Kondu leading them.

Periappa looked uncomprehendingly at them from his place on the thinnai.

'I am going to report you all to the police. What kind of atrocity is this? What right have you to break the gate of our house?' Kesavan shouted angrily.

'What right do you claim to have to keep my father locked up in your house?' Kesavan turned to look at where the voice had come from.

Soundaram was standing there.

Kesavan felt rage overcome him.

'I know how fond you are of your father. Perhaps these people do not know how you pleaded with Appa that this man, your father, should not be allowed to stay in our house and should be put in some *ashram* for the destitute. I know your true face. Please, go away.'

'It is not proper that you have his father under your custody here. If I give a written complaint to the police, they will file a case of abduction and put you behind bars. I know the laws of the land, I know everything,' said Kondu.

Soundaram stood near his father and softly called him, 'Appa!'

Periappa looked him up and down.

'I am your son, Soundaram, come home with me,' said he.

'How can you take him to your house when you have a house with so many other tenants? If he stayed in a big house, it would be easy for visitors to come and see him,' said Kudai Sarangan.

It was very obvious that he was not keen on letting Periappa move out of their street.

What guarantee was there that Soundaram would share the gains with others?

'Kesava!' He could hear Amma calling him.

He went in.

'What is it, Amma?'

'If Soundaram wants to take his father home, let him. Let us not have any trouble now. When Appa comes back, you tell him all that has happened. He will understand,' said Amma.

Kesavan thought for a minute. Will Appa accept this decision? Was it right to let Periappa go when Appa was not around?

'I am positive that Appa will not approve of it. I think it is wrong to do something that might displease him,' said Kesavan as he came out again.

They were all crowding around Periappa. Some of them bore trays of fruits.

'Put the fruit trays in front of Periyavar. Take his blessings,' said Soundaram.

The fruit trays were placed in front of Periappa.

Suddenly Periappa got up. He, who had been silent all that while, spoke now.

'I am not going anywhere. I shall stay here.'

28

*K*esavan's Periappa had categorically declared that he would not leave his brother's house and go anywhere. He had gone inside the house as if to prove his point, the crowd dispersed.

Soundaram stayed back.

Periappa sat in the hall leaning on a pillar.

The way he suddenly spoke with determination, rejecting the crowd as if they were all of no consequence and came in and sat there in the hall, took Amma by surprise. Kesavan, too, saw his Periappa in a new light.

Soundaram was cribbing to Amma, 'Chithi, you tell me, shouldn't he be living with me? Isn't he my own father whose last rites, only we are entitled to do? Now, he comes and sits here in your house...'

'Why didn't you think of all this earlier?' asked Amma.

'Only now have I realised that he is a great man, do you mean to say that all those who came here now were fools?'

'Who ever can call them fools? They are clever, know how to make hay while the sun shines,' said Kesavan and laughed.

'Soundaram also knows the art of survival,' joined in Amma with a smile.

'What is wrong with that? When he had money, he let us starve. Now, when it seems as if the divine power is here, showing us a way out of our misery, what is wrong in using him to earn some money for us?' said Soundaram, his voice decibel going up.

'Take him home if he will come with you,' said Amma. Soundaram went and sat near Periappa.

'Appa, Don't you recognise me?' he said in a voice that was oozing care and concern. He gently held his father's hand.

Periappa shook his hand off. But he did not say a word.

'I am Soundaram,' still no word from Periappa.

'Somebody has done some witchcraft,' said Soundaram.

'You averred just now that he was a saint. How he could be subjected to witchcraft and all that...I don't understand,' said Kesavan.

'I am taking him home with me,' said Soundaram in a firm voice.

'He refuses to go anywhere, how will you take him?'

'I know how! Some basic lessons that I have learnt from my lawyer-boss.'

'I have some knowledge of law, he is not a minor!' said Kesavan.

'He is not in his right senses, I'll put in a claim that you are holding him here by force.'

'And hold him for what gain? We don't intend to make some Samiyar of him and earn money!'

Periappa stood up. He glared at Soundaram.

'I am Soundaram, Appa. Your son,' said Soundaram in a sudden burst of affection and ardour.

'I know. You want to show me up as a Samiyar and make money. I shall not let that happen. I will stay here, in my brother's house. He is a gentleman,' said Periappa.

That he spoke so clearly and firmly made Kesavan drown in wonderment. That meant – Periappa had all along been quite conscious of everything! He had been watching all that was happening around him as a mere spectator. How strong he must be mentally!

'When you were rich you let us starve. Can't you help us make some money at least now? This would be the atonement for all your sins.'

'One sin cannot atone for another,' said Periappa.

'What sin will you be committing now.'

'Committing the sin of deceiving people. I am no saint or any such nonsense. It was my brother who, even when he knew that I would not be of any use to him, brought me here from the temple and since then has been feeding me. I know how you reacted the day I came here. I was watching all the fun.'

'I reacted strongly to all the treachery you had committed against us, was that wrong?'

'No, that was not wrong. But don't try to make a fake *Samiyar* of me now. If projecting me in this way, begins to rake in the lucre for you, then there is the further danger of you believing that, I am, indeed, a great man. I cannot handle that!' said Periappa, smiling. He appeared to be a new man altogether.

'Why do you say, "I cannot bear it"?' asked Kesavan. Periappa looked at him for some moments. Then he said, 'You are a college student. Have you heard of JK?'

'You mean J Krishnamurthy?'

'Yes! Annie Besant tried to make of him, a Krishna of this *Kaliyuga*. But when he was of a certain age, he felt he could not handle it and moved away from the Theosophical movement. That he has been able to preserve his sanity and mental balance to this day, is because of this decision. Go, see in your temples. See God feeling suffocated, smothered as he is, by the murmurs of mantras by the devotees and all the anointments that he is made to suffer. And why are all these done? Ultimately, they amount to gratification of petitions asking for this or that.... All under the name of *Bhakthi*. I don't want to be a party to this fraud.'

Kesavan looked at Periappa with a heart full of new found joy. They say he was very learned. Could all the accusations heaped on him be true? Why did he forsake his wife and children? Did he never realise that what he did was wrong? They say he went around with a white woman. Who was she?

That he should finally come to sit at the entrance of a Kumbakonam temple and beg, seemed to be so contradictory to his nature! Or was there no contradiction at all? How did this sudden transformation happen? He must be lying. Had he, now, decided to be a participant instead of staying a mere spectator?

How will Appa accept this new incarnation of Periappa? No one wants the images formed already in his or her mind to be demolished. Appa knows only the Periappa who, sitting at the gates of the temple, was begging for his food.

But this Periappa is one who speaks of Annie Besant and JK. He criticises our fake devotion with a subtle occidental type of humour.

Will Appa like this new, transformed man?

29

$\mathcal{A}$ big surprise awaited Kesavan when he woke up the next morning. Periappa was standing in the veranda outside the room where he had been sleeping. He had never before come upstairs. Kesavan went to the veranda.

'You are surprised, seeing me here?'

'Yes!'

'When your father came back last night, I told him all that had happened here. So he deported me from the thinnai downstairs to this floor upstairs! I thought it would be a better proposition to accept this physical elevation than to get upgraded to become a saint....You also need some company, don't you?'

'What did Appa say?'

'About what?'

'Wasn't he surprised to see you talk like this?'

'If one has crossed the age of sixty, nothing in the world ever surprises him.'

'Will not a life that holds no surprises be a boring one?' asked Kesavan.

'It depends on one's attitude to life. If every little thing fills a person with wonder, then he is very lucky. He is one not contaminated by education. Take me, for instance, my sitting outside the temple, being brought home here, some people here trying to make a saint of me…. I see all these as preordained. I do not accept that anything happens by chance. But I cannot claim to have any faith in God either.'

'Do you say that you believe only in fate?'

'No! Behind all actions there is an intrinsic logic. But, this goes beyond a cause-effect reasoning. It could be a, "method in madness." Your father and I were born in the same family. Why should I be what I am and your father so different? I cannot say he is different. Perhaps our life-styles were different. But, basically we have been honest to ourselves. I do not know much about you. From your conversations I surmised that you were a Communist and you have been suspended from your college now. This does not surprise me. This rebel element expresses itself in one form or other in our family, every generation, identifying our underlying individualities.'

He went on speaking. Amma's voice calling out to her son came up from the ground floor.

'Your Amma seems to want you. Go down.' He said tightening his dhoti around his waist.

Appa was seated on the swing; Kesavan could see that he was deep in thought.

'A telegram for you!' said Amma.

'From where?'

'From your university.'

The telegram was in Appa's hands.

'What is it about?' asked Kesavan going near Appa.

'You first have a wash and drink your coffee,' said Appa

Periappa came own the stairs.

Kesavan had is coffee and came and stood by his father.

Now the telegram was with Periappa. He laughed and told Kesavan, 'It says that your father should express his regret about your having participated in the strike. It wants him to stand guarantee for your good conduct. Then you will be readmitted into the college.'

'What nonsense is this?' said Kesavan as he took the telegram from his Periappa and read it over.

'I don't think you are going to achieve anything by studying Tamil, nor is there any need for it. Just go to Kodavasal, as Appa has been suggesting and take care of our lands there. That is enough. We don't want Appa to go through the humiliation of going to your university and apologising,' said Amma.

'All those who were suspended would have got similar letters. We cannot let this pass. I shall go to the university...' Kesavan had not finished his sentence when Appa said, 'Go there and do what?'

'We may come up with a joint action.'

'Keep talking of joint action and all that! All the other parents would have given their letters of regret and got their sons back into the college, by now. I know this country much better than you!' said Periappa. Kesavan felt that there could be truth in what he said. Yet, it was difficult for him to swallow that bitter truth.

'Look here, if you want to continue with your studies there, you can go to the university, apologise or do whatever it is that you want to do. I shall, certainly not go there. If you want to discontinue your studies, that is also all right by me,' said Appa.

'Should we submit to injustice?' asked Kesavan.

'The meaning of these terms, justice, injustice and all such keep changing according to the times one lives,' said Periappa with a wry smile.

'Don't try to be smart!' said Appa angrily.

'Then, you tell me what Dharma really is? In the Bhagavat Gita the Lord took the blame on himself claiming that he was both righteousness and anarchy! So, if we worship the negative, it would still amount to worshipping God. That was why there came a delegation then, holding aloft a flag in support of wrong doing. We have had enough discussion on what is right and what is wrong. That's why I tell you, you can apologise to the authorities if you want to continue with your education. Or else, you can preserve your self-respect and stay at home! The choice is yours. Both actions can be justified and validated,' said Periappa.

'Justify our action and convince whom?' asked Appa.

'Isn't there within each of us, something called conscience, constantly putting us on the dock? I am talking about that,' said Periappa.

Somebody calling out Appa's name could be heard from outside.

Kesavan went outside.

There at the entrance stood Lakshminarasimha Iyengar; the man who had been accused of misbehaving with the servant maid and had got out of the scrape with the help of his economic strength. Kesavan remembered that the man had been angry with Appa, for Appa had openly condemned his action.

Why was he here now?

With the advocate were Kondu and Soundaram.

'Is your Appa in?' asked the Vakil.

By then Appa and Periappa had also come out of the house.

The visitors came in.

'There is a complaint against you. Soundaram wanted to go to the police but I stopped him and said that we should talk it over with you and come to a compromise,' said the Vakil with a smile.

His betel-stained teeth gleamed.

'What is the complaint?' asked Appa.

'He says that you have forcefully kept his father in your custody, put in legal terms, you have committed abduction, a crime punishable by law.'

'I am here of my own will and pleasure. It is 47 years since I became a major,' said Periappa.

'So, there was a time when you were a "minor"?' the Vakil asked with a mischievous smile punning on the word 'minor' which referred to a rake as well.

'Sure! But I am a major now. However, you seem still to be a minor, with 'keeps' in every street of the town, right?' asked Periappa in an even voice.

'Shut up,' shouted the Vakil.

'No! No show of anger, please! Vakils should not lose their tempers. Who told you that I was held here against my wishes? This blessed son of mine? The other day he was suggesting to Kesavan's mother that I should not be given a shelter here. Then, he wanted to make a saint of me to make some money. I have disappointed all of you. So you take it out on us like this, isn't this the truth?'

'He is not in his right senses,' said Kondu.

'So you think that all that I speak now is not said consciously, is that what you imply?' asked Periappa with a laugh.

'What will you do taking this man with you, Soundaram? This man has begun to talk, so it will be utter waste to try doing anything using him,' said the Vakil in a tone of sympathy.

'Exactly! If I had maintained my silence, the hordes of devotees could come up with various interpretations for my actions. Now that is not possible!' said Periappa.

'I would say you are one who does not know how to take advantage of situations. If you had agreed to become a mahan, at least you could have helped your family to come out of its stringent situation. Nothing is as effective as ochre robes,' said the Vakil.

'Perhaps wearing khaddar would help,' put in Appa who had been silent until then.

30

$\mathcal{T}$rivandrum Fast Passenger arrived at Kumbakonam station at 7.45 pm.

Kesavan got on the train. Chidambaram was 56 miles away. It would be a three and a half hour run. Sometimes it stretched to four hours

They say travelling to Delhi and other such faraway places took more than 52 hours. Kesavan wondered how people ever had the patience to go on such long trips.

Opposite him sat a family of three, a father, a mother and a daughter. The daughter must have been around eighteen years of age. She had sort of out-grown the *Pavadai-dhavani* outfit that she was wearing. He thought that she must have been a pampered child. The girl had bright eyes, giving one the impression that she was a clever one.

She had an English book in her hand – a Thomas Hardy book – that surprised Kesavan. Perhaps it was a textbook.

No, *Tess of the D'Urbervilles* was not likely to be a textbook.

Kesavan, who had not considered Hardy to be a very great writer, had been asked to read, *Tess* and *Jude the Obscure* by Krishnan.

Noticing Kesavan's glance resting on her book, she opened it and started to read it.

Kesavan had come to know that all other students except him had apologised and got back into their colleges.

If there was going to be any further study for him he had to tender an apology as well.

He had to make the choice. Appa refused to make any suggestions. It was Periappa who stressed on him that ideals or opinions had no relevance in practical life. He did not say anything more about his personal life.

He felt he had accepted Periappa's suggestion only because what Periappa said suited him.

What would suit him? Continuing his studies – a university life? Perhaps he was not prepared to disobey the rules and forfeit that opportunity.

The VC will write 'admit' on a slip of paper with a smile of triumph. With whatever institution you clashed, the final victory would be the institution's.

All that a clash or confrontation did was to foster one's ego; it ended there. Establishing that one had an individual identity seemed to be the sole aim of all struggles.

'Are you going to Madras?' Kesavan turned round when he heard a voice. It was the girl's father addressing him.

'No. I am going to Chidambaram.'

'You are at Annamalai?'

'Yes.'

'Engineering?'

He would go up in that man's esteem if he said 'engineering'. But if he owned up to Tamil, the conversation might stop right there. Was it necessary to give a reply? It appeared as if the gentleman was eagerly awaiting his response.

The girl also seemed to be interested in the reply he might give.

Though her eyes were on her book, he felt her attention was on the conversation her father was having with him.

'You like Thomas Hardy?' asked Kesavan.

If she had been really reading, she would not have heard him. He had spoken rather softly.

'What did you ask?'

'I study Sanskrit,' said Kesavan

'I thought you said something else.'

'No.'

She gave him a hard look. Her eyes were beautiful. As Kamban described, 'Wide as a sea.'

'Your name?'

'Pillai Perumal.'

The girl could not control her laughter.

'Why do you laugh?' chastised her mother.

'My name must have made her laugh. Isn't it a strange name?'

'There was once a great Vaishnavaite named Pillai Perumal Iyengar. I am also a Vaishnavaite. My name is Gopalarathnam.'

'My father's name is even stranger,' said Kesavan.

'What is that?'

'Pattinathu Mudali.'

'Do people have such names?' the girl's mother raised a doubt.

'We belong to a very conservative Vaishnavaite family. Haven't you heard of Pattinathu Mudali?'

'Sure! Sure! I have heard of him,' the father nodded his head in an attempt to stress the affirmative.

'There seems to be no connection between the way you are dressed and the name you claim to be yours,' said the girl.

'Sh...Sharp tongue! Keep quiet!' said the mother pretending to be angry.

'It is all right! Let her say what she wants to, what makes you say that?'

'The name conjures up in my mind a mama in dhoti worn the traditional way and sporting a caste mark on the forehead...but you, dressed like this in pants...' not knowing how to proceed she stopped mid-sentence and laughed.

'What is your name?'

'Kannamma.'

'She was named Komalam, we call her Kannamma,' elaborated her father.

'Komalam is a nice name, why not call her by that name?'

'You think, modern girls appreciate good names?' said the father.

'That's true. My father calls me by the name Perumal. I like to be called that. You take the name 'Perumal' a hundred times a day, wouldn't that be sufficient to ensure your place in Vaikuntam, the Vaishnavaite heaven?'

The gentleman was not sure if there was a teasing tone in Kesavan's voice or the boy really meant what he said. He agreed to Kesavan's words with some reservation.

'What do they call you at the university?' asked the girl.

'They call me Pillaival!'

The girl laughed loudly.

'Pillaival would take on an entirely different meaning,' said the girl's father.

'What meaning?'

'It would mean a different caste!'

'Does the name Pattinathu Mudali indicate that the man was a Mudaliyar? So what if the caste changes? Don't people decry mention of the word 'caste' nowadays?'

'They do. But who forsakes his caste? What is your *gotram*?'

'Miss Komalam! Do you like Thomas Hardy?'

'My name is Kannamma.'

'Komalam is a nice name too, isn't it? My grandmother's name was Komalam.'

'Is your native place Kumbakonam?' asked the girl's father.

'Yes!'

'On which street do you live?'

'Varaha Kulam Street.'

'Varaha Kulam Street? My brother-in-law lives there. There...
There...' he did not finish the sentence.

'Yes, tell me.'

'I have not heard of anyone by the name Pattinathu Mudali living
on that street.'

'Why don't you like the name Komalam?'

'It is not an urban name, not usually used in cities.'

'The consort of Lord Sarangapani is Komalam and you dare to
call it rural or small townish?'

'Don't mind her, I asked for your gotram, you have not yet given it.'

'Have you read *Jude the Obscure*?'

The girl looked at him, surprise in her eyes.

'Why do you look at me so strangely?'

'You seem to know the titles of English books!'

'How can you say that, Miss Komalam? Should I not be knowing
them?'

'Don't call me Komalam. My name is Kannamma.'

'What if he calls you that?' said the mother smiling.

'I don't like it!' the girl said angrily.

'Why do you want to know my gotram? Your daughter doesn't
like me,' said Kesavan with a smile.

'Don't you pay any attention to her,' said her mother.

'Give me your address. Next month I...'

'No!' said the girl giving a vehement shakes of her head.

'Don't mind her!' said the mother.

'See! Your daughter detests me, why do you compel her?'

'Shall I tell you the real reason? Your name is funny, you are funny
too! In addition to all that, your father's name is the funniest of all!
Pattinathu Mudali! My God!' she said and laughed loudly.

'Chee! Shut up' her mother shouted at her.

'I am sorry!' said the girl.

Even as she apologised, she bent down and pulled out a vessel
from under her seat.

She pinched a bit off the dough from the vessel and put it into her mouth.

'What is that?' asked Kesavan.

'The dough to make Appalams,' said the mother.

'When I was a young boy, they would make appalams in the hall of my house. I have seem some of the grannies eat the raw dough then. My mother never ate it. My mother would tease them saying that to have a taste for raw dough was, indeed, strange,' said Kesavan laughing.

'Ok. Stop it,' said the girl in anger.

The train stopped at a station.

It was Mayavaram.

Some eight or nine people rushed into their compartment.

Kesavan felt that he should not have teased the girl all that much. He was looking out of the window.

'Kesava! Are you going to Chidambaram?' He turned round to see who was calling him.

It was his father's friend, the astrologer Vaduvur Mama. He could not recollect the gentleman's name.

'What did you call the boy?' asked the girl's father.

'Why do you ask? I called him Kesavan.'

'Do you know him?'

'How can I not know him? We live on the same street.'

'Is his father's name Pattinathu Mudali?'

Vaduvur Mama laughed loudly.

'What kind of name is that? Pattinathu Mudali? Who told you so?'

'That boy, he told me.'

'What's it Kesava? You have been teasing them? This boy's father is a great scholar of the Sastras, named Nadathur Srivathsan. He lives in Sannidhi street in Kumbakonam.'

'So, that gentleman is the boy's father!' the girl's father could not hold back his surprise. Kannamma gave Kesavan a smouldering look.

31

$\mathcal{K}$esavan did not expect to have such an awesome reception at the Chidambaram railway station: the warden, a sub-inspector and a couple of policemen!

As soon as he got off the train, the warden who was standing some distance away, pointed him out to the sub-inspector and said, 'That is the boy, come on!' They came towards him. Kesavan turned his head to look at the compartment from where he got off. The girl was sleeping.

That the girl did not witness the scene that would have shown Kesavan up as a hero disappointed him a little.

'What makes you give me this honour, sir?' Kesavan asked the warden.

The warden showed him a sheet of paper. It was a typed apology letter.

'Where is your father?' asked the warden.

'He has gone to Calcutta.'

'Calcutta?'

'Yes. To attend a function in connection with my sister-in-law's niece attaining puberty.'

The warden interrupted him. 'That's enough, I know you are a Brahmin. Take all these tales to the VC. You got a place in the hostel conning him, didn't you?'

'It is getting late, sign the paper, Thambi. We have got to be going,' said the sub-inspector.

'You are the only one left to sign, all the other sheep are in the pen,' said the warden with a smile.

'How on earth did you know that I was coming by this train?'

'Simple, my dear Watson, Your letter to Krishnan.'

Would Krishnan have betrayed him? Krishnan did not appear to be one capable of any act of treachery.

'Don't suspect Krishnan. I casually asked him when you were coming. He does not lie and the simple fellow that he is, he gave me the answer,' said the warden with a triumphant smile.

'Sir, it is getting late for us, if he signs the paper, our job will get done, right?' said the sub-inspector wearily.

Kesavan put in his signature on the paper.

'Good! You may go now,' said the warden.

Kesavan knocked on the door. A sleepy-eyed Krishnan opened the door.

'Welcome Rebel!' said Krishnan with a mischievous smile.

Kesavan silently put his box under the cot and sat on the bed.

'Have you signed the apology?' asked Krishnan.

Kesavan nodded.

'I thought you wouldn't.'

'Have I come down in your esteem now?'

'Not really, it was just a thought.'

'I shouldn't have got into this protest putting my stakes on these clay horses.'

Krishnan smiled.

'What is this smile for?'

'Heroic words well-spoken!'

'You are a cynic!'

'Ok, shall we go to sleep? It is rather late,' said Krishnan.

Next morning, Krishnan told him, 'I need your help.'

'What help?'

'My cousin's friend is coming here to Chidambaram to attend some medical conference. She is a doctor. You have to be Krishnan for a day or two.'

'What nonsense is this?'

'She has not seen me. My cousin has asked me to take her around the city, Nataraja Temple etc etc...I cannot do it. Please help me. She has not seen me, so it should be no problem.'

'You want me to impersonate?'

'This is no impersonation. You will be of service to a dear friend, that's all.'

'Why not I say that you are not in town and I, your friend, shall be escorting her around the city?'

'Why can't you be Krishnan for just a day?'

'What if she suggests that we come to our room?' Kesavan raised the doubt.

'Just introduce me as Kesavan! Simple!'

'What, exactly, is your problem?'

'None at all. Some of you go on strike, do all sorts of things claiming that you are Communists. I accept, that as your identity. I prefer to be without any special identity whatsoever. I, with sharpened nails, wish to watch you all, like God.

'James Joyce?'

'Right, you are well read. That is not important now.'

'The point made is that you claim to be God – that is your identity.'

'What identity can God have? If He can be specified, He cannot be God. Neti. Neti, neti etc, etc... Tell me, please will you help me?'

'When is she coming?'

'She is already here. You will meet her this afternoon at two o'clock at the Sastri Hall. She will be waiting for you there. Here is her photo.'

Krishnan handed over a photo to Kesavan.

'She is good looking.'

'Say it again, that's your reward. You have another advantage as well. But that depends on how you use the opportunity.'

'I don't understand you.'

'She may fall in love with you,' said Krishnan and laughed.

'Don't be silly!'

'You are not able to hide the tinge of excitement in your voice. The entire world lives on hope! Survival of the handsomest!' said Krishnan and laughed louder.

At two o'clock Kesavan was punctually at the entrance to Sastri Hall.

The morning session of the conference was over and many of the delegates were coming out of the hall. They were all elderly or middle-aged. None of them was really young. It was also possible that Krishnan's cousin was a middle-aged doctor and had sent a photograph of herself taken during her younger days.

Some young doctors were coming in small groups. Who among them was Doctor Subhadra?

There she was! Indeed a beautiful woman, no one could dispute that. The photo had not lied. She seemed to be in some serious discussion with another woman.

Kesavan walked towards her.

'Dr Subhadra?'

'Yes.' Her look seemed to ask, 'Who are you, come to meet me?'

'I am Krishnan.'

'Krishnan?' her look and voice seemed to say that she was not convinced.

'My cousin...her name? Yes! Padma? Padma had written to me.'

'I see...'

She was not yet convinced.

'If you are busy... That's alright...I can come later.'

She was taking leave of her friend with a smile.

She looked at him once more silently.

This was a new experience for Kesavan. He was quite uncomfortable. He regretted getting into this predicament.

'Is the conference over?'

'I had visualised a different kind of Krishnan.'

'I don't understand you.'

'Ok. Forget it!'

Would Padma have given Krishnan's photo to her? But, when the doubt had occurred earlier to Kesavan and he had asked Krishnan about it, Krishnan had assured him that he had never in his life been photographed.

Or, perhaps, Padma had described Krishnan to this lady.

'How did you visualise Krishnan to be?'

'Let that be. You come with me. I shall leave these papers in my room and then come with you.'

'It is our VC's order that no trace of any man be seen near the women's hostel. There was even a strike protesting against it. I shall wait for you here. You go and put these in your room.'

'We are guests. Your rules will not apply to us,' said Subhadra.

'I am not a guest. It will be valid for me.'

'Ok, then, you stay here. Can you get a cycle for me from somebody? That will make my trip quicker. How long can you wait?'

Waiting would be a problem. He looked around. Eapen was riding his bicycle.

Kesavan raised his voice and called out to Eapen.

Eapen stopped.

Kesavan went up to him.

'Please lend your cycle for five minutes. She wants to go to the ladies' hostel and will be back soon.'

'Romancing?' asked Eapen with a wink.

'Don't be silly! She is my sister, come here for the medical conference.'

'Really? I am sorry! Keep the cycle in your room. I shall come and take it later.'

He pushed the cycle and went towards Subhadra.

'You are resourceful.'

She was back in five minutes, just as she had said she would.

It did not look as if she had applied any fresh make-up.

'You are very quick,' said Kesavan.

'Depends on circumstances,' said Subhadra.

Kesavan was not sure if the present circumstances were advantageous to him or not.

'Give the cycle to your friend,' said Subhadra.

'He said he would take it later. I shall keep it in my room on our way out.'

'There may not be any need for that. There comes your friend.'

Eapen was coming towards them.

Rascal, he is back, just to take another look at Subhadra!

32

'Good evening!' said Eapen to Subhadra.

'Good Evening!'

'I am Eapen.'

'Thank you, Eapen. It was your cycle, right?'

'That's nothing. A small help for a friend's sister, that's all.'

Subhadra looked at Kesavan. Kesavan was looking up at the sky. It did not look as if any help would come from the sky, though.

'We are all brothers and sisters of the world. That makes you my brother too.'

'That is right,' said Eapen.

'What is there to see in Chidambaram?' asked Subhadra.

'How can you say that? The Nataraja temple is world famous.'

'And then?'

'Kesavan may know more about that. Kesava, what else is there to see?'

'Kesavan may not. He even forgets who he is at times.'

'Is that so?'

'It could even be schizophrenia.'

'You are a doctor, you can treat him, can't you?'

'I intend to. So, thank you, Eapen.'

Eapen's disappointment, at her cutting him off so cursorily, was clearly evident on his face.

He took his cycle and walked some distance away.

'Shall we go, Krishnan?' asked Subhadra.

'I am sorry!'

'For what?'

'This was Krishnan's idea, not mine.'

'This is, indeed, schizophrenia. I have no doubt about it. When shall we start the treatment, Krishnan?'

'Krishnan is a very shy man. He doesn't like to meet strangers, especially if they are ladies. It was he, who...'

'Stop it! You be Krishnan. I like it that way,' said she laughing.

'You must meet Krishnan.'

'You mean Kesavan?'

'Please...'

'Ok, let us go, meet him. But you must not tell him about what happened here.'

'It is not fair.'

'What is not fair, your meeting me as Krishnan?'

'I am sorry.'

'Come, let us go;

Krishnan was not in the room. Where could he have gone?

There were only two places Krishnan visited. One was the library. The other was the bookshop. That shop was in Annamalainagar. It was owned by a Tamil writer.

Kesavan thought that they should first look for Krishnan in the library. He was not there. Then they went to the bookshop. Krishnan was sitting there. The owner was not around.

Kesavan thought that Krishnan was taken aback at this surprise encounter.

'This is Miss Subhadra,' Kesavan introduced her to Krishnan.

'Namaskaram, Mr Kesavan,' said Subhadra.

Krishnan gave Kesavan a look.

Kesavan was not all that keen to meet Krishnan's eyes.

'Krishnan said that you were his close friend. So, I thought it would be nice to meet you.'

'Didn't you go to the temple?'

'What's there in a temple? Meeting you is equal to a visit to the temple, I would say,' said Subhadra.

'I see.'

'Is not Subrahmanya Iyer in?' asked Kesavan.

'He's asleep.'

Subhadra began to browse through the books in the shop.

It was clear from his face that Krishnan was not happy with their coming there.

'Do you have *The Prisoner of Zenda*?' asked Subhadra.

'I wouldn't know,' replied an irritated Krishnan.

'Have you read the book?'

'No.'

'A very interesting book!'

'I don't think sustaining the interest of the reader is the yardstick of good literature,' said Krishnan.

'I did not say the book had any literary merit,' said Subhadra with a smile.

Krishnan gave Subhadra a once over.

'I was wrong,' he said after a few moments.

Kesavan could very well understand why she was making references to that particular book. Impersonation was the core idea of that novel. Krishnan might have read the book or at least have heard of it. But, Kesavan thought that it would not have occurred to him to relate the book to Subhadra's words.

'There are no medical books in this shop,' said Krishnan.

'Oh, I see! I thought I would find a book on schizophrenia here,' said Subhadra laughing.

Krishnan who had all along been seated, got up stretched his limbs and asked, 'Why schizophrenia?'

'I think the two of you are very close.'

'So?'

'So, you are both afflicted by schizophrenia. You are both Krishnans as well as Kesavans. It becomes difficult to say who Krishnan is and who Kesavan. Identity crisis!' said Subhadra.

Krishnan smiled. Kesavan did not expect this reaction

'I don't see any problem in this,'said Krishnan.

'I don't have a problem but you seem to!' said Subhadra.

'What does it matter by what names we are called? We give ourselves names of Krishnan, Kesavan or Subhadra, only to distinguish one from another. There ends the matter. Aham Brahmasmi!'

'I thought you were a patient of some mental disorder, but your disease seems to be one caused by philosophy!'

'Are you not going to Chidambaram?'

'This experience is more interesting than a visit to Chidambaram. Oh, but you don't like anything to be interesting, do you?'

'It is literature that transforms something interesting into an art,' said Krishnan.

'Do you mean to say that it should stop being interesting?'

'Only the experience of finding it interesting will be there. There will be no art there...as the verse goes, "The great wooden elephant got lost in the wood, the great elephant hid the wood!"'

'Krishnan, who is there?' asked a voice from within the shop.

It was Subrahmanyam.

'Kesavan and his friend.'

'I thought I heard a female voice?'

'Yes!'

Subrahmanyam came out. Tying his dhoti tightly at the waist he looked at Subhadra, his glance appraising her from head to toe.

'Are you here to buy any book?'

'Do you have a copy of *Prisoner of Zenda*?'

'A movie was made of that book, did you see it?'

'The movie must have been better than the book.'

Subrahmanyam sat on a chair. He must have been around forty years of age. He had on thick-framed glasses. His voice was bass, like he was speaking from the bottom of his throat.

'What is it Kesava? I don't get to see you here, nowadays?' asked Subrahmanyam.

'His name is Krishnan, not Kesavan,' said Subhadra.

'What do you mean? Is this Krishnan?'

'What does it matter who we are? We just take names Krishnan, Kesavan or Subhadra to distinguish ourselves one from the other. Aham Brahmasmi!' said Subhadra.

Subrahmanyam looked at the three, one after another, uncomprehendingly.

'You are Subhadra?' he asked after a few moments.

'I could be even Krishna,' said Subhadra.

'Why not Arjuna?' asked Subrahmanyam.

'Why not? Or Ardhanareeswarar – half-man, half-woman,' said Subhadra.

'I don't have a clue as to what you are saying,' said Subrahmanyam.

Kesavan told him what had happened.

Subrahmanyam smiled.

'I now understand why you asked for that particular book. But it is not as simple as that. Krishnan likes being Kesavan and making Krishnan of Kesavan But I am not sure if it is acceptable to Kesavan.'

'This is not an issue of who likes or dislikes to be whom, I just tried to help Krishnan, that's all,' said Kesavan.

'Don't you delude yourself with all those explanations? Forget it. Why did you make a sister of me?'

'The conversion of any relationship with a woman into a sister acts as a barrier to all uncomfortable, wrong ideas that might arise in one's subconscious. This sister complex is a great obsession of our

Tamilnadu. It becomes the main theme of most of our Tamil movies,' said Subrahmanyam laughing.

'You are now, trivialising it, making it appear vulgar,' said Kesavan cut to the quick.

'Ok, let us all go to Chidambaram. Will you join us Mr Subrahmanyam?'

'Sure! There is a coffee shop where you get very good coffee, called Maruthi Vilas in Chidambaram,' said Subrahmanyam.

33

$\mathcal{T}$rue to Subrahmanyam's words, the coffee at Maruti Vilas was very good.

'You have a good taste when it comes to food,' said Kesavan to Subrahmanyam.

'I enjoy good literature, too. One who cannot enjoy good coffee may not be able to enjoy good literature either,' said Subrahmanyam.

'That's a tall claim,' said Kesavan.

'Are you interested in music?' asked Subhadra of Subrahmanyam.

'No, not at all,' said Krishnan laughing.

'Why do you answer on his behalf?'

'I know he is not interested in music. I also can guess why you asked the question.'

'Appreciation of any one art is enough, that may lead to an interest in other arts. Shakespeare says that a man who is not interested in music will not hesitate to commit even murder. But I cannot bring myself to kill even the ant that bites me,' said Subrahmanyam laughing.

'We don't have to kill the ant that bites us. The way we push it off us is enough to cause its death!' said Subhadra.

'You mean to say that ants also have masochistic tendencies?' asked Kesavan.

'That is the problem with Kesavan. He will torture us with use of jargon based on his half-baked knowledge of psychology,' said Krishnan.

Kesavan was irritated at this remark of Krishnan. Krishnan was not one to put down anybody. Why was he talking like this now?

'Who was it that used the term schizophrenia, you or Kesavan?' Subrahmanyam asked.

'I did. Perhaps Krishnan will call my knowledge of psychology half-baked, as well,' said Subhadra with a smile.

'I am sorry,' said Krishnan. Kesavan thought that Krishnan had realised the inappropriateness of his remark. Perhaps his own question whether ants had masochistic tendencies could have also been to impress Subhadra; just to make her have a good opinion of him.

He had asked the question to exhibit his knowledge of psychology; what answer did he expect to get?

'Shall I ask you something?' asked Subhadra of Krishnan.

The four of them came out of the hotel.

The street was crowded. In addition to the milling crowd, bullock carts manoeuvred themselves, dexterously weaving their way through.

'I don't know why this place is so crowded today, even more than usual.' said Subrahmanyam.

'Festival in the temple,' said a passer-by, who must have heard Subrahmanyam's question, even as he gaped at Subhadra.

'What about our visit to the temple?' asked Subrahmanyam.

'This is something that our special guest has to decide. If you are going there, I shall not join you,' said Krishnan

'That would be intimidation,' said Subrahmanyam.

'No, it is not intimidation. It is just looking for an opportunity to escape. He has not yet answered my question,' said Subhadra.

'The question has not been asked yet,' said Kesavan.

'I asked him if I could voice a question. But he has not given me any answer for that,' said Subhadra.

'Ask away. He will answer you,' said Subrahmanyam.

'He has not opened his mouth at all,' said Subhadra.

Krishnan continued to walk silently. Perhaps he knew what the question would be. Or, at least he had made a shrewd guess.

'Ok! Why did you not want to meet me? I have asked my question, though you have not give me the permission to ask it.'

'That is his nature. Is it wrong to be content with the number of people you already know and show no interest in making new acquaintances?' asked Subrahmanyam.

'Then he could have just stayed away. Where was the need for him to send somebody else as Krishnan. He was under no compulsion to please anybody, was he?'

'Are you sorry that I came to meet you?' asked Kesavan.'

'That is not the issue. If you want me to tell you that I was happy you came to meet me, okay, I shall say that, I am very happy to have met you, but...'

Krishnan and Subrahmanyam smiled at her words and this made Kesavan feel a little uncomfortable. He decided to move away and go on his own. The cheek this girl had! She takes such liberties and thinks she could discuss him with others as she wants.

The crowd was gathering strength. Taking advantage of this, Kesavan moved away and began to walk in the opposite direction. The others did not notice this.

The crowd was heavy at the entrance to the temple. After debating for a minute whether he should go in or not, he decided not to.

Kesavan felt he should not have appeared so naïve before Subhadra. She was a clever girl, no doubt.

Arrogance seems always to accompany cleverness. Perhaps, it was this arrogance that made cleverness more attractive.

Could he honestly claim that he was not attracted by this kind of smartness?

Subrahmanyam was an arrogant man too. Very learned, no denying that. But his arrogance was the kind that decided all others were ignoramuses and he had to explain even the most trivial of things to them. His was, 'You are an idiot, what can I do?' kind of patronising arrogance.

Kesavan had bought a book of verses by TS Eliot from Subrahmanyam's shop. When he met Subrahmanyam the next time, he had asked Kesavan, 'Did you read the book?'

'Yes, I did. Some lines are just brilliant.'

Subrahmanyam merely smiled without saying anything.

'What is this smile for?'

'Your comment that the poems were brilliant amused me, I couldn't understand what you meant by that.'

'Why?'

'Never mind.'

'Tell me, what was wrong in what I said?'

'There was nothing wrong.'

'Then why that smile?'

'As far as I am concerned, a good poem is an experience. I don't feel I can see any separate quality of brilliance in it.'

'Just as you say good coffee, or good *dosai*, why cannot you describe a poem as being "good"?'

'Goodness is something different. I have never said any coffee was brilliant. The term, 'good' refers to some innate feeling that has become part of me, my experience, something that cannot be seen as separate from me. When it has been so assimilated, how can it be qualified and categorised? When I am very hungry, I can satiate my hunger with reading a good poem.'

'I cannot believe it.'

'You don't have to. I know that you will not be able to comprehend my claim.'

After this Kesavan had not seen Subrahmanyam for quite some time.

Krishnan told him that the man had suffered a great loss in his book-selling business.

Kesavan was not surprised.

Will a bookseller who asked all the students who came to the shop to buy books, 'You buy these books, do you think you can understand them?' make any profit? Kesavan had no clue as to why Subrahmanyam went to the trouble of running a bookshop. Perhaps it was to get books for himself to read; or it could even be to make others believe that he was engaged in some trade.

By the time he finished his dinner and went back to his room it was past ten. Krishnan was reading a book.

Krishnan asked Kesavan, 'Why did you have to go off like that?'

Kesavan did not reply.

'Was it because Subhadra spoke the way she did?'

'What do you mean?' burst out Kesavan angrily, his voice raised.

Krishnan did not say anything. After staring at Kesavan for a few minutes he went back to his book.

Kesavan lay down on his cot.

Krishnan also switched off the light and lay down on his bed.

After a few minutes Krishnan asked, 'Are you in love with her?'

'Don't be silly.'

'Then why this display of anger? I think you have given her more importance than she deserves. You are impulsive.'

'No, No! I lost you. I did not know where to look for you in that crowd. So I went to the temple.'

Krishnan was silent. His silence was a clear indication that he did not believe what Kesavan had said.

A while later, Kesavan asked, 'What do you think of her?'

'Nothing.'

'I think she is arrogant. What we did was wrong, I agree. But I didn't like the way she, instead of getting angry with us, started to tease us. Anger would have been justified but sarcasm? I don't like it at all!'

Krishnan continued to be silent.

'Why are you silent?'

'What do you want me to say?'

'You are arrogant in a different way. Subrahmanyam in yet another way.'

Krishnan got up from his bed and switched the light on.

The sudden brilliance of the light made Kesavan's eyes flinch.

'Why the light now?'

'Only to see if it was you.'

'I don't see what is so funny.'

'I thought the Kesavan I was familiar with was a mature person. Now you are talking like a moon-struck adolescent boy. To put it in Tamil...'

'Don't even try, switch off the light and go to sleep.'

'Look Kesavan, Think about whether your going off in a huff at what she said was right. Did you not see that it could be a display of your inferiority complex? And the way you are talking now..."Subhadra is arrogant, Subrahmanyam is arrogant, I am arrogant..." My god! The impact she has had on you seems to have made you go crazy, makes you rave now, I can't believe this! Do you like her so much?'

Kesavan did not reply. Krishnan's words singed him. True; he had gone crazy.

What would Subhadra have thought of him?

To want to know her opinion is in itself a sign of his madness. He had never before met any beautiful, intelligent girl. This was his first experience.

That he believed her words had angered him...perhaps, that was also part of this crazy love-sickness!

Why couldn't he be like Krishnan without any of these foolhardiness? Was that his natural self?

'Do you know what Subhadra thinks of you?' asked Krishnan. Kesavan was silent.

'Don't you want to know?'

'No!'

'Ok, then let us go to sleep.' Krishnan put off the light and went back to bed.

'What does she think of me?' asked Kesavan after a while. Krishnan's mild snores answered him.

34

$\mathcal{K}$esavan was up very early the next morning and was struggling with *Senavaraiyam*. Krishnan had tried in vain to pick up a conversation with him and had now settled down to writing in a notebook that was his diary.

Kesavan had a doubt that Krishnan might be writing something about him.

'Are you writing about me?' asked Kesavan.

No answer from Krishnan.

'I think it is about me – you are writing, isn't it?'

Krishnan said with a smile, 'Some people when they are bored, like to do crossword puzzles. Your interest is *Senavaraiyar*, for me it is my diary.'

'Are they all the same?'

'Yes.'

'What did Subhadra say of me yesterday?'

'That she loves you, does that make you happy?'

'Don't be silly!'

'Then what do you expect me to tell you?'

'Wasn't it you who said yesterday, "Do you know what she thinks of you?" Now tell me what she thinks of me.'

'That you are as yet an unspoiled mother's virgin boy.'

'Is this a compliment?'

'I wouldn't know, I just repeated what she said. She may come again to see you. Ask her if it was meant to be a compliment or not.'

'Why would she wish to see me again?'

'Once again, the answer is "I don't know". I just tell you what she told me. Perhaps...'

'Perhaps?

'She's in love with you.'

'Don't be silly.'

'This time when you said that, your voice didn't sound angry. It appears to have made you happy. Good luck!'

The hostel watchman Isakki came there just then. He was an old man who claimed he was not yet fifty years old. He had been with Annamalai University right from its inception. Perhaps he had been around when it was still Meenakshi College. The students respected him.

'Thambi! There's a girl here come to see you, it's not good,' said Isakki to Kesavan.

'Why do you say "not good"? It is a good-looking girl, isn't it?' said Krishnan.

'I didn't mean the girl. I said it was not good for a girl to come looking for a boy.'

'Then go, tell her that it is not proper for her to come here visiting, and ask her to go away,' said Krishnan.

'It is just that she says it is important. She is from somewhere outside.'

'Wait! I am coming down,' said Kesavan.

After Isakki left the room, Kesavan got changed into appropriate outdoor clothes.

'You look smart,' said Krishnan.

Kesavan ignored him.

'Ask her, don't forget,' said Krishnan.

'Ask what?'

'Ask whether unspoiled mother's virgin boy is a compliment or...'

'Or what...?'

Krishnan laughed.

'What are you trying to imply?' asked Kesavan.

'Or whether she has any objection to your being like this.'

'Like being what?'

'An unspoiled mother's virgin boy!'

Kesavan stared at him. He had never before heard Krishnan talk in this manner.

Was he jealous? Of whom? Of her or him?

It may not be any surprise even if he was jealous of her. He was well aware of Krishnan's weakness. When once, he had casually referred to it, Kesavan remembered him saying that he believed only in spontaneous, energetic sex. That was, perhaps, why his voice when it spoke the words 'unspoiled mother's virgin boy' was so harsh, as if it was some self-inflicted punishment.

'Ok. Forget it. Don't ask her anything.'

'Why, because she didn't say any such thing?'

'Shut up!'

Kesavan felt that Subhadra had also taken some care in dressing up, before coming to see him.

'Why did you go away yesterday, without a word to anyone?'

'I think it is better we don't talk about that.'

'Why not?'

'What brings you here?'

'I go back to my town this afternoon, so I thought I would bid you goodbye.'

'What need do you have to say goodbye to an unspoiled mother's virgin boy?'

'I don't understand.'

'Krishnan told me that you said that of me.'

'Nonsense! Why would I say anything like that? Why does Krishnan make up all these lies? Is he around?'

'Forget it. Come, let us go.'

They walked silently for a while.

'Why does Krishnan tell you that I said something I never did? I don't understand the psychology behind it.'

'I understand him.'

She gave him a long, hard look; she smiled. A few moments later she asked, 'May I ask you what you have understood?'

Kesavan did not reply. He walked silently on.

'Perhaps Krishnan is jealous of you.'

'For what?'

'For not being like you.'

'What do you mean – like me?'

'You wish to wrench a compliment from me?'

'Only because I am not sure...'

'Not sure of what?

'Of whether you really mean half the things you say...'

'I am not like you...impersonating, calling all the girls you come across – sisters – suddenly making off without a word to anyone...'

Her face had turned red as she spoke those words. Kesavan felt he had made her angry.

She moved away a little from him

'Vanakkam Kesavan!' said Nallaperumal who had just come there.

'Vanakkam'

Nallaperumal's eyes were on Subhadra.

'I am not his sister, I am his friend,' said Subhadra.

Nallaperumal looked uncomprehendingly at Kesavan.

Kesavan walked fast without any comment. It was clear from his fast pace that he was angry.

'Does it mean you are angry if you walk fast?'

'Who are you and who am I? What have we to do with each other?'

'Is it a rhetorical query or...?'

'I shall not argue with you. I was wrong to pretend that I was somebody I was not. I am sorry. I think it would be better for both of us to put all that behind us and part as friends.'

'Why do you get so angry?'

'Then why do you tease me in front of all and sundry? I was wrong to introduce you as my sister. '

'Don't you have any sense of humour, Mr Kesavan?'

'You call this, a sense of humour? Who knows what that boy Nallaperumal will go and tell others?'

'What can he say? Kesavan was seen with a girl and she is not his sister, isn't that all? Am I not your friend?'

'Are you?'

'I am. I like you very much. But don't fly off into imagining that I am in love and all that.'

'When a girl tells a boy that she likes him very much what else can it mean?'

'Should it mean love? That is why Krishnan...' she stopped half-way through the sentence.

'Yes, go on.'

'He must have called you "unspoiled mother's virgin boy". You are an incorrigible romantic!' Subhadra took his hand in hers.

35

Kesavan was deep in thought. He may have been attracted by some girls while in Kumbakonam. But it could not be called love.

Was this love? This state of being smitten by Subhadra?

After Subhadra had gone back to her place, he had written three letters to her.

He had received no reply.

He did not want to talk about it with anybody, especially Krishnan. Krishnan had, from the very beginning, taken on an air of sarcasm while referring to anything about the episode.

Why had she not written to him? He remembered what she had said, 'Don't imagine that I am in love with you.' What did she mean then?

She had held his hand the other day.

He recollected how his mind was filled with joy and undulated with emotion like the Cauvery in spate.

She had stared at him for some minutes.

He felt as if she was embracing him with just that look.

She had said, 'Ok. What now?'

'Let us go back. I shall write to you.'

She did not reply. She was silent.

'I cannot speak but I can write,' Kesavan had said.

'Our Tamil boys are capable of both speaking and writing or at least good at one of these like you say you are. That is all they are capable of, though.'

'What do you mean?'

'Writing and speaking or writing or speaking, that's all. Come, let us go.'

'What are you trying to say?'

'I have dropped the terms of respect when I address you. You have not, that is what I mean.'

Kesavan wondered. Was she disappointed in him? What did she expect from him? Why did she make that remark about Tamil boys? Krishnan's words also crossed his mind – 'unspoiled mother's virgin boy.'

He was a virgin.

Many boys went to Chidambaram, to shed their virginity.

Once Dharmavinayagam had called him to go with him saying, 'It is not wrong, come.' But he had refused.

What was behind his refusal? Was it on some moral grounds or was it mere fear? He did not want to go into any research of that issue now.

When he was at school, he had gone with his parents once to Oppiliappan Koil.

At the thinnai of the house they had visited, an aged person was sitting – a leper who had lost part of his limbs. He was the elder brother of the head of that house. His mother had said, 'Immoral man, if you consort with low class girls, you can expect to earn just this.'

His appearance had created a mammoth fear in him. Loose conduct will lead only to this. Perhaps it was this fear that made him refuse to go with Dharmavinayagam the other day.

What would Subhadra have expected from him? If it had occurred to him that day that she might have had a different kind of expectation, his opinion of her would have also been something very different. He would not have penned all those letters to her.

Was he merely a platonic lover?

What had kept him stick to tradition when it came to sex?

Krishnan came in. For the past few days he had not been talking to Kesavan in the easy manner he had as he did earlier. Kesavan thought that the change had come from the day he went out with Subhadra.

Was Krishnan also attracted to Subhadra? Human mind was, indeed, strange! Nobody could be made a snapshot and confined to a frame.

Krishnan held a letter in his hand. He gave Kesavan a smile.

'This is from your friend,' said Krishnan.

'Who is my friend?'

'Subhadra.'

'Is the letter for me?'

'No! It is for me. Subhadra is going to America.'

'I see.'

'Want to read the letter?'

'No, thanks.'

Krishnan sat on the chair. He tossed the letter onto the table.

Then, he bent down and caressed his knees.

Kesavan put on his shirt and got ready to go out.

Krishnan slanted his head, lowered his spectacles and looked at Kesavan.

A slight smile played on his face.

'Are you going to eat?'

'No.'

'Kesava, you are a fool!'

Kesavan did not give any answer.

'What happened the other day?' asked Krishnan.

'Which day?'

'You know exactly which day I am talking about.'

'Nothing happened. Does that make you happy?'

'That is your problem.'

'What is?'

'You were not able to judge that girl.'

'I don't care.'

'Stop bluffing.'

'I am going out.'

'Are you not coming to your class?'

'No.'

Krishnan was quiet for a while. Kesavan put some clothes in a small bag.

'Where are you going?'

'To Pondicherry.'

'Pondicherry? What takes you there?'

Kesavan did not give him any reply. He picked up his bag and went out.

Only when he was out in the open did it occur to him; why did I mention Pondicherry?

The desire to visit Pondicherry had been at the back of his mind for quite sometime now. His mentor back home Subrahmanya Iyer, who had never held anybody or anything sacred, had often spoken to him very highly of Aurobindo. He was in the habit of going to Pondicherry to have a darshan of Aurobindo.

'It is good for all of us to have a pet superstition. Aurobindo is mine,' Subrahmanya Iyer would say.

'What is new in Aurobindo's teachings?'

'Nothing. He has said the same things that Vallalar had earlier talked about, the language he uses is English, that is all! I have not seen Vallalar. I have the opportunity to meet Aurobindo once a year. So, why not use it?'

Why did Aurobindo come into his mind, suddenly now?

Neither Aurobindo, nor Subrahmanya Iyer was alive now.

What was wrong in his joining the Aurobindo Ashram?

He felt it was ridiculous. He could write a book on, 'From Marxism to Aurobindo's philosophy'.

Marx and Aurobindo – did they both not try to create Utopias? One was an economic utopia and the other a spiritual utopia. One was the monopoly of labourers, the other the highest state of the soul.

Why should he be thinking on these lines?

Subhadra had rejected him and will be flying off to America. Was that the reason?

No, No, No! Tamil grammar did not permit the usage of any word more that three times.

He did not care for Subhadra. He was not worried about anything whatsoever. He would spend his life incognito in Aurobindo Ashram. It was said that yoga had given Aurobindo's body his golden sheen. Subrahmanya Iyer would also often say, 'What a colour the man has! All aglow and shining!'

Will he become like that in another twenty years? How will Subhadra look then? Middle-aged, mother of three, flabby at the waist...if he happened to see her then...! What a perverse kind of imagination? Had he felt cheated to that extent?

It was a great surprise. A girl, whom he had come across suddenly, briefly, could she make such an impact on him!

This was madness. It will be proper to go back.

What if Senavarayar refuted the commentator or did not? If he did not study Tholkappiyam, will it mean the world's end?

Nothing had any meaning. The only thing that mattered in life was death. What the existentialist claimed was true. Macbeth also holds the same view. 'All sound and fury end in nought.'

Why should one look for meanings?

After he had composed a thousand verses the wisdom that dawned on Nammalwar seems to be just this. What remains finally is emptiness.

Chee! What madness is this! Was it wise to seek meanings in things?

Senavarayam, Nachinarkiniyam, Kaivalya Navaneetham, Muthu Kumaraswamy Pillai Tamizh, Prabhulinga Leelai, Naidatham, Virali vidu Thoothu....

Chee! Was life just these, so trivial?

Aurobindo Ashram would be a better place to be in. Identitiless, one can hold out the plate for food, eat and spend one's time in researching about nothingness.

But eating had to go on. Stop hunger, you stop breathing. Hunger was the ultimate truth!

The ignorant say hunger and Siva are different; if only you realised hunger was Siva!

By the time he reached Pondicherry and stood at the door of the office of Aurobindo Ashram, he was at that state of spiritual extreme, having realised Siva completely.

He was very hungry. He could not be sure if it was the rumbling of his stomach or the cry of his soul that was heard from within him.

He told the official at the office, 'I want to become a member of this *Ashram* community.'

The one behind the table sized him. The man must have been more than fifty years old. His kurta, pyjama, thick-framed spectacles, a broad face and hair brushed front to back...all pointed to the fact that the gentleman was a Bengali:

'What do you mean?' He asked.

Kesavan repeated his plea.

'Where are you from?' Though he spoke in English, Kesavan felt that his form of addressing him had changed from the respectful plural to the singular.

'Annamalai University.'

'A student?'

'Was a student, I have now lost interest in studies.'

'What are your interests now?'

'Spirituality.'

There was a trace of a smile on his face.

'Have you eaten?' he asked after a few moments.

'No.'

'Go, eat and then come back here. We can talk.' Kesavan wondered how the gentleman could make out from his tired face that he was hungry.

'Where do I go to eat?'

He wrote on a small piece of paper where he should go.

'Thank you. I shall be back after I have had my food.'

Just as he had expected he was served on a plate. The rotis and vegetables that he was served could not be called tasty. It was bland with less salt.

If you wanted spirituality, you had, perhaps, to give up spice and salt.

Having had his meal, he went back to the office.

Another gentleman was there now.

He was very old; must have been around seventy; the voice dripped with compassion.

'I want to enrol in this ashram.'

'You?'

'Have you run away from home?'

'No, I was a student. I lost interest in studies. I felt as if Aurobindo was beckoning me.'

'Did he come in your dream?'

He wondered what reply he should give to this question.

He recollected having read somewhere that those who seek spirituality have always something to relate about their dreams. But how was he to know if this gentleman was teasing him or putting the question to him in earnest?

'Yes,' he replied in a weak voice.

'Go, finish your studies first and then come back.'

'The learning seems to be of no use. The more you study the more ignorant you become.'

'Ignorance at its boundary leads to knowledge.'

'I don't understand you.'

'Accepting your inability to understand is the first lesson towards knowledge.'

'Will I not be allowed to join this ashram?'

'Complete your studies. Your ignorance will mature. That would be the time for you to come here.

'Do all those who come here, come with those qualifications?'

The gentleman did not reply.

Kesavan stood there silently for some time.

Then, the gentleman whom Kesavan had met earlier came there. He saw Kesavan and with a smile asked, 'Have you eaten?'

'Yes, I have.'

'This boy wants to join our ashram,' said the gentleman with the thick-framed glasses.

'So, he tells me. I told him that he should come back after he has completed his studies.'

'I am very much interested in the philosophy of Aurobindo,' said Kesavan.

'Can you put Aurobindo's philosophy in just one word?'

'Over soul.'

'And what does that mean?'

'Man's soul has to evolve. Evolution is not something that concerns only the body. I did read all of it. But I could not understand it.'

The two gentlemen looked at each other. Kesavan wondered if they had not themselves made any sense of the enigma.

'What did you not understand in that?'

'I could not understand what it was that I had to understand.' The two exchanged glances once again.

'When can I join here?'

'Look here. It is not all that easy to become a member of this ashram. All your property...do you have any...? All of it must be made over to the ashram. Are your parents alive?'

Kesavan stood there silently for some time. Even spirituality ends at a point where material property is!

'Why would they want my property? Will not my person be seen as some wealth?'

They did not make any comments. They stared at him for a few moments.

'What do you say?'

'About what?'

'About my becoming an inmate of this ashram.'

'We have said all that needs to be said. Now it is your decision,' said the Bengali gentleman.

Kesavan came out of that place.

36

*A*mma was a little surprised at Kesavan's unannounced arrival. She had just finished her lunch and was on her way to the backyard to wash her hands when she saw him come in. She stared at him for a few seconds, her surprise evident in her eyes,

'What is it Kesava? Why this surprise visit?'

It looked as if Appa was not at home.

Periappa was asleep on the thinnai.

'Have you had your bath? Will you eat now?'

'Yes, I will eat.'

He washed himself and sat down for a meal.

'I don't think you have any holidays now, why, then, are you here?'

'I wanted to see you.'

'Don't give me that story. Tell me, what is the matter?'

Paruppu thukaiyal, vatral kuzhambu, keerai masiyal, thakkali rasam, vellarikkai pachadi... Nothing in the world could ever equal Amma's cooking.

'I got tired of hostel meals. We eat potatoes or eggplants every single day. I came home to have a proper meal.'

'I don't believe you. You have never been fussy about food. Why do you fib?'

'Where is Appa?'

'Some scholar has come to Veerachi Mama's house. They say he is very well versed in our traditions. Veerachi Mama came and invited Appa to go and meet him. It is two hours since Appa went there, he is still not back.'

'Where has he gone?'

'You remember Therazhundur Mama from Iyengar street? The visitor is staying there.'

'Isn't Therazhundur Mama a huge fraud?'

'Chee! Don't talk like that.'

'Come dawn, you see him playing cards at Porter Hall. Do you know how many people he has cheated in those card games? Now he is into meeting saintly men and discussing Vedanta. How is it that Appa went to his house? Appa knows all about that man and yet...?'

'I cannot argue with you. I don't have the energy for it. You tell me, why have you come here all of a sudden? Do you need any money?'

'How is Periappa?'

'He is no bother. Soundaram tried his best to make some money out of him. But Periappa stood his ground and did not yield an inch. He stays here.'

'Does he talk now?'

'Not really. Just a word or two, to the point, that's all! It is really a marvel that he is able to stay silent all the time staring into vacant space!'

'He was talking to me.'

'Not any more. You see a smile suddenly appear on his face, but you will not know what caused it to appear. After all his jaunts, now....'

'You are wrong. He never had any fling. He went in search of truth.'

'Go! You too go on a search!'

'I am about to do just that. That is why I have come away from Chidambaram.'

'What do you mean?'

'I am not interested in these studies, Amma.'

'Then what do you want to do?'

'I feel it is all so meaningless.'

'What are you talking? First, you ran around calling yourself a communist, they sent you out of the university. Now you come and proclaim that everything is meaningless, like a madman. You want to go Periappa's way?'

Kesavan went into the hall without saying anything.

Amma followed him.

'Why don't you say something?'

'I am confused, Amma.'

'Are you not feeling well?'

'I want to go upstairs and get some sleep. We'll talk later.'

He went upstairs. His room was as he had left it. Nobody came there. But it had been regularly cleaned. – 'Just sweep, don't disturb the books there' – this must have been Amma's order to the maid. He lay down on his bed.

Never before had he slept like that. When he woke up, it was five in the evening. He had slept for nearly six hours.

He felt more at ease.

He came down. Appa was in the hall on his easy chair deeply engrossed in a book.

He lifted up his gaze when he saw Kesavan. He asked in English, 'What is your problem?'

'None at all.'

'Is it that you do not want to study?'

'It is not that, suddenly…'

He stopped mid-sentence.

'Tell me.'

'I have lost interest in everything.'

'And the reason is…?'

'I don't know.'

Periappa came in and looked at him with surprise.

'He says he's not interested in anything. He has come here, leaving his studies half-way,' said Appa to Periappa.

Periappa sat down on the floor resting his back on the pillar.

Amma called to him from inside the kitchen, 'Come here.'

'What is it Amma?'

'Just come, I say.'

'He went in. Sathyabhama Patti was standing there, a ladle in her hand. She must have been around seventy-five years old.

'Sit down,' said Amma. He sat down.

Sathyabhama Patti waved the ladle round in front of him to remove evil eye.

'What madness is this, Amma?'

'What is madness? Your turning up suddenly claiming to become a samiyar, you who were so active all along! What does that mean? Except that someone has cast their evil eye on you?' said Patti.

'See how it pops!' said Amma.

'Who told you that I was going to become a samiyar?' asked Kesavan.

'What does it mean when you say that you have lost interest in everything?' said Amma.

Kesavan came out of the kitchen into the hall silently.

Periappa asked with a smile, 'So, the evil eye has been removed?'

'Yes.'

'They tried to make a samiyar of me, they didn't succeed. Now, you become one!' said Periappa the smile still on his face.

'Are you teasing me?'

'Shall we go upstairs? We can have a talk,' said Periappa.

Kesavan looked at his father. Appa was silent. But it appeared that he was agreeable to Periappa having a 'talk' with Kesavan.

The two went upstairs.

'Let us go up to the terrace,' said Periappa.

'Why?'

'You will get good breeze there.'

Kesavan's house was rather a big one. The height of the house seemed to enhance the stature of one who stood on the terrace.

'Look how beautiful everything looks from here! Sarangapani sits, in his lofty mansion, after having usurped the house from the poor Someswara. Do you know the story of Someswarar?'

'Yes, I do.'

'Both the temples of Someswarar and Sarangapani must have stood on the same expansive premises. Perhaps the Siva's temple was big and the Perumal's smaller. Perumal must have come seeking shelter. Gradually expanding his territory, ousting Sivan...thus goes the story; a very interesting one too. It must have happened during the Chola period. If the king was a Saivaite he would cast the Perumal's idol into the sea; if he was a Vaishnavaite he would put the Vaishnavaite caste-mark, Namam, even on Murugan's forehead!'

Kesavan was silent.

'Not that I know anything about its veracity, I go by the popular version of the story. Sivan and Perumal could have just exchanged places. Nothing ever is permanent. If this is the lot of the Gods what are we to say of mere human beings? Okay, tell me why this detachment that you feel now?' Is it failure in love?'

Periappa's question came like a slap on his face. He was startled and gaped at the older man.

'Why do you ask this question?'

'I was also like this. I lost interest in everything. I'll tell you the reason now. It was love failure. I had been married then, also had a child. The entire episode in retrospect appears so funny.'

Kesavan did not say anything. A couple of pigeons flew away from the middle of the Saranagapani temple tower. He stood watching them.

'Tell me, was it love failure?'

'I don't know if it was unrequited love. Perhaps I had imagined the love. But this is what happened.'

Kesavan narrated the entire episode beginning with Subhadra and ending with his visit to the Aurobindo Ashram.

Periappa gave him a patient hearing. He did not interrupt Kesavan's narration with any questions.

When Kesavan had finished, there was just a streak of smile on Periappa's face.

'I think I have been a thorough fool,' said Kesavan.

'One needs to have all sorts of experiences. That is the only way for a person to assure himself that he is, indeed, human. You should not be sorry about anything that happens in your life. Ponder on your experience, standing apart, being non-judgemental. It may not be possible for you now. Perhaps when you reach my age you will be able to. At that point, you will see the experience as something interesting.'

'What has been your experience?'

'I was the first in our family to get English education. Then came an early marriage, I felt I was a stranger to all that was happening around me. As far as 'that woman' was concerned, she got attracted by my composing a poem about her. If I had had the time and opportunity, I might have written an entire epic! I think all epics got written that way. I think all the plays of Shakespeare must have been written for his 'dark lady'. All I could come up with was just a poem.

'But as far as she was concerned she was a married woman. What she had with me was just an affair. This came as a shock to me. You went to Aurobindo for solace. I went to Annie Besant. Both are similar. I tell you, don't go on experimenting with your life like I did. What has happened to my ultimate goal that I went after? Thinnai! That is why I tell you. Life is great, sacred...forget all these inanities. We have been given a life here, in this world. Let us have trouble-free lives. There is nothing so worthy in this life that warrants either tormenting our minds or feeling ecstatic. It is all just a state of mind, so listen to me. Go and complete your studies and come back with your degree.'

'Are you an existentialist?'

'Nonsense! I am talking so seriously and you are still hanging on to mere words and phrases!'

They came down. Appa was asleep.

37

'*I* go to Chidamabaram tomorrow,' said Kesavan to his father.

He was reading *The Hindu*. Periappa was reclining against the pillar, gazing at the sky that appeared as an awning in the open space in the middle of the hall.

Amma who was passing by with the milk pot in her hand, turned around to look at him.

'You plan to study?' asked Appa.

'Yes,'

'Right then, go, but not tomorrow, go the day after.'

'Why? Is it not an auspicious day tomorrow?' asked Kesavan with mockery tainting his voice.

'I don't know about that. There's the ritual of giving raw bananas to the priest tomorrow. It is your uncle's death anniversary.'

Periappa turned his gaze sharply at Appa and asked, 'Did he do the death rituals?'

'Who else is there?'

Periappa gave Kesavan a smile.

Kesavan did not understand the meaning of that smile. It could have meant many things.

It could have been, 'Do you believe in such rituals?'

Or, 'If you don't believe in them and yet are prepared to do them to satisfy your father, then you must be prepared to make many more compromises. My sons will not do the rites for me when I am gone, I hope you will do them.'

These thoughts assailed Kesavan's mind as he went upstairs.

That he had done the rites for Chithappa had been quite an issue then.

'An only son! And he has to do them first for his Appa or Amma and instead he does it for a Chithappa who is only his father's half-brother...' The people of the Agraharam were up in arms against this.

But Appa was not concerned with any of these opposing voices. Chithappa's susequent death anniversaries were, however, not performed at home.

The annual ritual got condensed to having a priest come home and take rice, raw bananas and money as alms. This, in a matter of speaking. was also a compromise. The compromise Appa made because Amma was not for doing any elaborate ceremony at home.

His father's father – his grandfather – must have been a very interesting person! He had three wives, with a son from each one of them, and all three very different personalities.

Could Periappa and Chithappa be said to have been different from each other? Both of them stepped out of the house to engage themselves in experiments. Periappa was 'learned'. Chithappa did not seem to have had much of that. Even so, he had the determination to insist that his funeral rites should be performed with his own money. He did not want to be a bother to others. This made him an individual in his own right, there could be no doubt about that.

'You seem to be in some deep thought?' Kesavan turned round.

It was Periappa.

'Nothing!'

'The people of this street wanted to make a saint of me, but the real saint is your father. Standing up to all those opposition, he made you do the funeral rites for his brother. What a great act it is!'

'I don't understand,' Kesavan drawled.

'What do you not understand?'

'Why did Thatha marry three times?'

'Three marriages and then right from Kodavasal to Nachiarkoil concubines...innumerable....There is nothing wrong if people take cudgels against Brahmins today. That community has done any number of such atrocities. But, if like your Thatha staying within the societal control, not going against the priests, Chithappa or I had also conformed, did not step out of conventions in defiance of them, we would not have been chastised as we are today. The mistake we made was we dared to come out of the community.'

'Are you justifying your actions?' asked Kesavan.

'Not really, you can take this as a kind of protest. Basically, your father is also like us. But at the same time, he is not one to burn his boats in the name of defiance. Did he not refuse to make money making a samiyar out of me? If he had wanted it, I would have even agreed to become the samiyar!

'Really?'

'He brings home one sitting at the temple gates and feeds him without any question. How many will you find like him? Why would I not act the part of a samiyar if he will make some money out of it? But I know for certain, your father will not descend to such lowly acts.'

Periappa's talking about his father touched Kesavan's heart strings. He felt his eyes getting moist. He walked silently to the balcony.

Two days later, when he returned to his university, a surprise awaited him.

Krishnan had vacated the room and gone elsewhere. Kesavan told the warden, 'Give me a separate room, don't bring another boy into the room now.'

'I cannot promise you anything.'

'But how was it that you have allowed Krishnan to have a room all for himself?'

'It got vacant, so I allotted him one. The other boy went away discontinuing his studies. But that apart, you tell me where did you abscond all of a sudden? You went away without any formal permission and now you dare talk to me about rules!'

'I had to go home on an urgent matter.'

'Shouldn't you have informed me? Krishnan also said that he did not know anything about it.'

'I had not told anyone. There was some problem at home. My father asked me to come urgently.'

'Ok, But don't repeat this habit of going away without taking my permission.'

The first period was *Kamba Ramayanam*. Ramaswami Pillai was an interesting professor. He enjoyed his own lectures. That was his speciality. While thus completely involved in his subject, his voice would falter; his eyes would brim; it was from that teacher that Kesavan realised that silence marked the height of one's appreciation

Yet the verses that he enjoyed in *Ramayanam* were debatable. He would find it difficult to appreciate the teacher going gaga over the literary merit of some lines that he thought were nothing extraordinary.

Moreover, it always surprised Kesavan that the most ordinary events of daily life could send Pillai into a sense of wonderment

'You enter a room and press a button and the entire room is flooded with light! How wonderful! It is all due to the great white man's brains.' He would exclaim excitedly.

'The white men are all gone, sir!' would chip in Subrahmanya Pillai.

'So what if they are gone? Their intelligence is something that will always be remembered. When King George VI died, I composed an elegy in Tamil. A fine specimen it was of that particular metre. But I could not find anyone to appreciate my poetry. The reason was the hatred our people had of the whites. It is all right to hate the whites;

but can that be the reason not to appreciate a good elegy?' Whether his students were inclined or not to listen to the verse, they would be subjected to a recitation.

As soon as Kesavan had sat in his class, Subrahmnaya Pillai asked him, 'Where were you for the last one week?'

'Some important business at home.'

'You went to choose a girl to marry?'

Krishnan smiled.

'Is there nothing else you can ever think of,' chided Kesavan.

Krishnan continued to smile.

Kesavan asked Krishnan, 'Why did you vacate our room?'

'So, Bhattar is not in your room now!' said Subrahmanya Pillai.

'No, he is not,' said Kesavan.

'Kesavan has gone all spiritual now. He went to Pondicherry and is now back with huge collections of spiritualism.

'He, a spiritualist?'

Then, Professor Ramasami Pillai entered the classroom.

Even as he began his lecture, he saw Kesavan and asked, 'How come you were not seen here for some days now?'

'Spirituality,' said Subrahmanya Pillai.

'What, spirituality?'

'Yes. Now Kesavan is a disciple of Aurobindo.'

'I don't understand. A communist and now he…how did this happen?'

'I am no disciple of Aurobindo. He is bluffing. I had gone home on some personal matter,' said Kesavan.

'Ok. Now let us get back to our lesson.' He opened the textbook.

'I told you yesterday, how beautiful this verse was! Viswamitran goes to Dasarathan to ask that Rama be sent with him to protect his Yagnya.

'He asks, "Of the four sons give me the dark-hued one" How is Viswamitran pictured here? As one who has done innumerable penances….How beautiful! How meaningful! Do you know how pregnant this line is? With the words separated in different ways it takes on different meanings! By one reading, it means one who did penance to get the worthy cow Kamadenu. Another interpretation would say that he tortured himself with various penances, meaning that Viswamitara, a Kshatriya and not a Brahmin used to such penances, had to go to unlimited trouble to do them....'

Ramasami Pillai did not stop with that. He tore the verse apart subjecting each word to rigorous surgical procedures. By the time he arrived at the last line of the verse, like a blind man regaining his sight, he reached the height of emotion and drifted into silence.

The bell rang. Ramasami Pillai had to be told that the bell had rung, to get him out of his trance.

As they came out of the class Kesavan asked Krishnan, 'Why? Were you upset with me and so you left the room?'

'I thought it would be good for you also.'

'What makes you say that?'

'I am glad you decided not to quit your studies half-way through especially, now that you are more than half-way through the course. You have only a couple of months more to finish.'

'Thank you, I have a few things to discuss with you.'

'I am not interested, please, just two more months. Concentrate on your studies. Don't torment yourself with other issues,' said Krishnan.

38

It was true that Kesavan had passed his exams with a first class, but no job seemed to come his way. There was only one vocation a Tamil MA could hope to find and that was teaching. Kesavan could not get even that.

He attended many interviews. He was asked many questions that had nothing to do with Tamil. He recollected how the Sanskrit teacher had once asked him what the chances were for a Brahmin by birth, learning Tamil to get a suitable job. It was his ardent desire to prove that man wrong. But, the doubt that all his efforts might become futile, began to gnaw at his mind. In one of the colleges, the college administrator was very candid when he commented, 'You, Brahmins, have raided all avenues – English, economics, maths...now you want to make your entry into Tamil as well.... Not bad at all!'

Though it was true that the man could not be faulted for what he said, Kesavan's paramount question was whether he should be made a victim of circumstances. He did not believe in the caste system. With their faith in their respective castes, people had universities to cater to their specific castes; Yadava University, Nadar University and so on.

Though never openly declared, there were some two or three universities that were pro-Brahmin. However, there seemed to be no vacancies in any of them.

Appa told him, 'Just go to the village. The lessees are out to cheat us. Show them that a Brahmin can also work in the fields.'

Kesavan was not sure if it was at all possible. He had grown up an urban animal. His dream was about entering the so many areas of the outside world that were waiting to be conquered. With such a mind-set would he be able to confine himself to a village? All his dreams about Independent India were turning to be just that – dreams. Congress ignored the freedom fighters and chose their candidates to stand for the election from among the affluent. The reason given for this was that the rich had more chances of winning. Dravida Munnetra Kazhagam that had initially come on the scene to fight for social justice, now entered the political arena. The lure of contesting the elections infected the Communists, as well, who had earlier spoken of an universal revolution.

The Communists hoped to create a mammoth labour revolution in India if they could be part of the assembly and the Parliament. It was at this juncture that the possibility of his getting a job in Tiruchi came by.

A friend of Appa was a retired engineer. After a dip in the Cauvery he came to Kesavan's house dripping wet. Appa who had been reading the newspaper, looked up and rose to welcome his friend.

'Please, come in, you seem to be in some tearing hurry.'

'It is about Kesavan's job.'

'Sit down, please.'

He sat down.

Kesavan came out of the kitchen and stood near the pillar.

'I have a friend in Tiruchi, who pretends to be a hard-core Brahmin-hater. That is his politics, nothing to do with us. He saw me at the Cauvery and told me that there was a vacancy in the National College, Tiruchi. They are on the lookout for a Brahmin boy to fill that post. Ask Kesavan to go there immediately and meet my friend. I shall give a letter of introduction. Kesava, come home with me. I shall write out a letter on my letterhead. Take tonight's boat mail and go to Tiruchi,' he said.

'Will you have some coffee?' asked Appa.

'No, I don't want any now. I came here in my wet clothes to give you this information. The boy is young! How long can he be without work? He shouldn't have gone in for Tamil studies. Anyway, what is the point in talking about it now?'

'Is your friend to be trusted?' asked Kesavan.

'Look here, he is a very influential person, a tobacco merchant, well-read in Tamil. Though he talks of Dravida Kazhagam and all that, his manager is a Brahmin, his cook a Brahmin.... He just talks ill of Brahmins in public and that too only in public meetings. When Periyar visits Tiruchi, he stays with this man. Will you go today to meet him?'

'I am tired of attending interviews, they always have their own candidate and make a show of these interviews.'

'This is a wrong attitude. You are not just another candidate, here. You are a Brahmin, that college is a Brahmin college. The job is yours. If my friend makes a promise he is sure to honour it. He got the son-in-law of this college correspondent a job in the Mettur Chemicals. He has the financial backing. He is the director of many companies. When I was in service as an engineer, I have helped him in many ways. He is grateful to me.'

Kesavan was not happy with this arrangement. Just because he had been born a Brahmin, he had to work in a Brahmin college. From time immemorial, the dictum that one should not cross the boundaries of caste – convention was what had been preached by the *Sastras*. He imagined how he would look, after another thirty years. With a thick tuft...thickness may not be possible...nature might harvest the hair.... The vision of him with the tuft declaring his caste, wearing the dhoti in the traditional way, caste marks prominent on his forehead, never neglecting the two-time ablutions, a sheaf of horoscopes in hand, running around in search of a non-Srivatsa gotra, Vadagalai bridegroom, for his daughter.... Caste could be sustained only in this manner.

Was Tamilnadu going to be inhabited by Brahmins, Mudaliyars, Pillais, Vandayars, Nadars and Padayachis? Was the ideal that all humanity belonged to one class, and one race to remain merely as s subject for poets to create poetry?

He must run away from Tamilnadu. Go to Bombay, Calcutta, Delhi? India is a vast country. Will not there be a place for him somewhere? But what was the guarantee that things would be different elsewhere?

'Stop mouthing all this nonsense? Don't dilly-dally. Start today,' said the engineer.

'It looks like working in the fields might be preferable as Appa keeps telling me,' said Kesavan.

'What an idea! If you go to work in the fields, you think the farmers will spare you? They will chop you off. Did you say any such thing?' he turned and asked Appa.

'Sure, I did. How much of a Brahmin are we? Do we beg for our food from seven houses every day? The *Vedas* say that a Brahmin should not accumulate wealth. Don't we have money in the bank? Yesterday a cousin of mine came here to visit me. I asked him where he was working. He said he was with 'Bata' company. A shoe shop it is! If one can work in a shoe shop, can't he till the fields?'

'You seem to be changing into an ardent disciple of Periyar,' said the engineer with a laugh.

'I am nobody's disciple. I felt it was futile to go against the tide. So I spoke thus, that is all!'

'A criticism of Brahmins came through in your voice. That is why I asked you if you too had become a disciple of Periyar?'

'Of course it was intended! The Vakil who molested a maid servant the other day, do you know what he is today? He is our MLA. He is called a Thyagi, because he claims to have gone to the prison. Don't talk about these things! It is better to keep our mouths shut!' Appa's voice reflected the disgust and hopelessness he was feeling.

'So, you think Kesavan need not go to Tiruchi, is that it?'

'Let him go, make the effort. If he gets the job, well and good. If he doesn't, I only said that instead of making a living with his mouth, let him use his hands.'

Kesavan was surprised at the change that had come over Appa. If one was honest and straightforward, perhaps it was the compulsion of the times that he become a cynic.

The engineer went away. After the meal Periappa – who was going back to his place in the thinnai, invited Kesavan to join him.

'What do you plan to do?'

'What do you suggest?'

'Working in a college is an attractive option. You will just be castrated in any government job. It is not feasible for you to work in the fields. That is, simply, empty talk.'

'Will I get the job?'

'You can only try. I can tell you this – You should never regret the choices and experiences you have had in your life. If, with the education that I got in those days, I had taken up a government job. I would have even won a Rao Bahadur or some such award and enjoyed a pension.... I didn't even need a pension. I had inherited so much wealth. I could have spent my life, reclining on an easy chair, enjoying the company of grandchildren....At least imagined myself to be having a comfortable life. But I don't regret not having had such an easy life. I think of all the varied experiences I have had and revel in their memories. I am happy. It is sort of interesting to go over all the hardships I went through at one point in my life. A life without mobility is no life at all.' With these words, he closed his eyes. Kesavan thought that the old man had gone to rest in the comfort of his memories. He went inside the house.

He left for Tiruchi by the night's boat mail.

The engineer's friend's house was in Thennur. It had a large garden. He went across to the door, stood outside it and called, 'Sir!'

A servant appeared. 'I have come from Kumbakonam. I would like to meet Aiya.'

The servant took the stairs that was near the wall and went up.

He came back after sometime and said, 'Aiya wants you to go upstairs.'

If this friend had met the engineer, at the Cauvery in Kumbakonam the previous day and was home today, he must have travelled by car, thought Kesavan. There was a Dodge parked outside.

Upstairs, he found himself in a large open area. Beyond that was a thatched hall without any walls. The engineer's friend was lying down on a wooden cot. You could not even call that lying down. He was resting on a pile of pillows. He was very fair-complexioned. He must have been over sixty years, of a very good physique and there were only a few grey hairs glistening here and there on his head. A lady – perhaps his wife – was massaging his legs.

'Come in, *Thambi*. So, you are Kesavan?'

'Yes.'

Kesavan expected that he would be offered a seat. But neither was he asked to sit nor did it look as if there was any seat for him to sit. If he at all sat, it would have to be on the floor.

'In spite of being a Brahmin, why did you decide to study Tamil?'

'It was my interest in Tamil.'

'Let me hear you recite the sixth verse from the 78th Canto of *Thirukkural*.'

Kesavan was quiet.

'You don't know?'

'Why do you tease this boy? Can all be as scholarly as you are?' said his wife with a tinge of pride in her voice.

'My grandson can do it, *Thambi*. That comes with learning them at an early age. Shall I ask him to recite it?'

'The child must be getting ready to go to school. Don't bother him,' said his wife.

'Are you familiar with *Thirukkural*?'

'Yes, a little.'

'Do you know who the author of *Thirumurugaarruppadai* is?

'Nakkeeran.'

Kesavan felt that his interview was taking place at the gentleman's house there and then.

The gentleman was silent for a while.

'Enough of your massaging, Ask two bowls of ragi porridge be brought up here for us.'

'I don't want any.'

'Why? Is it that you don't like ragi? It is good for your health. Drink it, Thambi.'

The ragi porridge arrived. Kesavan managed to drink it with some difficulty.

'Right then, I'll call and talk to the man in charge at the college. You go and meet Sudarshan Iyengar tomorrow.'

'Sudharshan Iyengar?'

'Yes, He is the college correspondent. Wear a *namam* when you go to meet him.'

'I don't believe in caste marks.'

'Wipe it away after you get the job.'

'I don't want to pretend that I have some belief, when I don't have it. Should I go to that extent...'

'Ok. If you don't get the job, don't blame me.'

'Why would I blame you? You are trying to help me, when that is the case...'

'Look here, Thambi, this college correspondent is a strange kind of man. If I ask him, he might give the job to even one coming from the Dravida Kazhagam files. But a Brahmin who will not follow the rigmarole that he is supposed to follow, will make him see red. That is why, I tell you, wear a namam when you go to meet him, but after you have joined duty there...'

'I cannot bring myself to do such a thing '

'You have an alternative. I can get you a job in St Joseph's College.

There is one Joseph Rajagopal there. A word from him is sure to get you the job. But on one condition...'

'What is that?'

'He was an Iyengar, now a converted Christian. He is looking for a groom for his daughter. He says he has no objection to an Iyengar converted Christian. If you don't like to be a Brahmin, why don't you become a Christian? Will your father agree to it? But the job is guaranteed.'

Kesavan was silent.

'What do you think of it, Thambi?'

'The issue is not whether my father will agree to this or not. I am not for it.'

'Don't you believe in religion?'

'This has nothing to do with religion. Do you think getting married is such a trivial matter?'

The older man stared at him silently.

'How old do you think I am, Thambi?'

'Fifty.'

His face brightened. 'No, I am sixty-eight, I got married when I was sixteen. She was ten. We have had a happy life together for fifty-two years now. It was an arranged marriage. What have we lost? You claim to be a reformer. Then marry someone from another caste. I shall be in the forefront solemnising it. The girl is beautiful. She is in her intermediate class now. At one stroke, you will get a wife as well as a job!' he said straightening his impressive form from his reclining position.

'Pardon me, I am not contemplating marriage, not just now.'

He stepped down from the cot. He put his hand on Kesavan's shoulder and smiled. Kesavan was not sure what the smile was for.

'Thambi, you refuse to wear the namam, you will not also get baptised. How do you think you will get a job, tell me? Ideals should always be only for preaching to others. Not for us to practise. Gandhi practised what he preached, what happened to him? He was shot. I reiterate this, wear a namam, recite the Gayathri, the job is immediately yours. That's all I can say,' said he.

'Right, I'll do that,' Said Kesavan

His acquiescence surprised the man.

'That is the way to survive,' he said laughing.

Next day Kesavan went to meet Sudharshan Iyengar. Iyengar must have been around fifty years of age. He had on a zari-bordered turban, dhoti worn the traditional way and the namam shone brightly on his forehead. Though Kesavan had told the engineer's friend that he would go to meet Iyengar, sporting a namam, he did not do it. Neither did he recite the Gayathri. Iyengar gave him a look as if he was appraising Kesavan.

'Hmm... is your name Kesavan?' he growled.

That must have been his real voice.

'Yes.'

'You are MA Tamil?'

'Yes. I got a first class in that.'

'You are from Kumbakonam?'

'Yes.'

He gave his father's name.

'You are his son? And you come with nothing on your forehead! Come, recite a verse from *Thiruvaimozhi*.'

Kesavan recited his favourite hymn of Kulasekhara Alwar, who marvelled at the fortune of Yasodha who got to witness the childhood pranks of little Krishna. The verse goes thus:

'Fresh butter was in the pot and you took a handful of it with your small hands. You were caught dipping your hand in the pot and then licking your fingers. When you got beaten with a rope, you stood there, red lips quivering, pleading guilty with folded hands, guilt writ on your face. Yasodha was, indeed, fortunate to see those handsome gestures and expressions you made, realise your divinity at the same time and enjoy eternal bliss.'

'Well done! A good choice! And you do recite it well. Ok, I shall phone the principal and speak to him about you. Don't join duty today, it is not an auspicious day. Come tomorrow and take charge. Have the caste mark. If you don't like the whole works, white and all, drop the *thiruman* – white – part; wear at least the red streak that is in the middle. Have you seen our vice-chancellor, Lakshmanaswami Mudaliar and his brother Sir Ramaswami Mudaliar? The *srichoornam*, the red streak, always adorns their foreheads, giving the faces a dignity. They belong to the Justice party. That does not prevent them from wearing the caste marks, does it? Ok, do you know how to say Gayathri? Come on, recite it!'

Kesavan recited the Gayathri.

'Go and join duty tomorrow.'

Kesavan, finally did land a job only because he was born a Brahmin, He belonged to the sub-sect Iyengar, he was from the Nadathur Iyengar clan and he could recite the Alwar hymns and Gayathri.

After Kesavan had signed in the register, a confirmation that he had the job, he sat crestfallen in the teachers' room. It was well that the moustached poet who had declared, 'Pappa, there are no castes' was dead and gone.

This was Independent India.

GLOSSARY

aio	alas, a term of regret
anna	elder brother
beedi	hand-rolled tobacco leaf for smoking
bhakthi	devotion, allegiance
charkha	spinning wheel used to make cotton thread to be made into *khaddar* – a symbol of Gandhiji's freedom struggle [to replace imported mill made fabric of the British Raj]
chee	an expression disgust
chithappa	uncle, father's younger brother
chithi	aunt, father's younger brother's wife
dosai	rice and lentil pancakes

darshan	sight in religious terms to see an idol to pay obeisance
gotram	sub-caste traced back to seven generations, an exogamous group
kaliyug	the present age, possibly the one that will see the end of the world as per Hindu Mythology
khaddar	*khadi*; hand spun cotton cloth. Wearing khaddar or kadhi became a key visual symbol of India's independence struggle from colonial rule.
mahan	enlightened person, ascetic
mama	mother's brother, term of respect: uncle
mantra	chant, incantations or recitations [of lines of prayers] of potent syllables
murasu cot	ornate settee, throne-like connotation
namam	Vaishnavite caste mark drawn on the forehead with sandalwood paste or with white clay and vermillion powder
namashkaram	greeting, literally 'I bow to the divine in you'
namaz	prayers offered five times daily by Muslims
Nila Thunga Sthanagiri	part of prayers describing the Goddess Lakshmi with beautiful breasts
paisa	one hundredth of a rupee.

pandal	podium, stage
poonool	sacred thread worn over the left shoulder and under right arm
periappa	father's elder brother, uncle
punkha	fan, here a suspended heavy cloth which is pulled and released to create a breeze
ragi	grain, millet especially used for porridge and so on
sambar	lentils stewed with vegetable [without onion for religious or ceremonial occasions]
samiyar	an ascetic, swami
Sangam Literature	Classical Tamil literature c. 300BC to 300CE Era
Senavaraiyam	A commentary on the Tamil grammar book *Tholkappaiyam*
sanyas	to renounce the world and take up the life of an ascetic
satyameva jayate	truth prevails
shastra	scripture [religious books including rules for living, rites and rituals]
shrichooram	a red caste mark on the forehead
tamasha	spectacle, public show

thambi	little brother, young man; a term of affection
thatha	grandfather
thinnai	veranda, sit out or porch
thiruman	the white part of the caste mark on the forehead
vakil	barrister
vaikuntam	heaven, abode of Vishnu
vanakkam	greeting
veli	a unit of land one veli = 7 kani = 6.43 acres = 2.6 hectares
veshti	cloth or silk garment (usually white) for men knotted at the waist covering the legs
yagnya	a prayer ritual, including offerings to a holy fire
yamaloka	abode of Yama; temporary purgatory
zari	golden or silver thread embroidery for garments and ornamental/decoration pieces